THE GEN-E PROJECT

A. MARIE ZELLMER

The Gen-E Project by A. Marie Zellmer

This is a work of fiction. All names, characters, locales, and incidents are products of the author's imagination and any resemblance to actual people, places or events is coincidental or fictionalized.

ISBN: 978-0-615-98648-7

Library of Congress Control Number: 2014904800

Cover design by Amy Young - amyyoungdesign.com

www.TheGenEProjectBook.com

First Edition

Printed in U.S.A.

For Jake

Take time to find the treasure wherever you go

To those who believed...

Dave, Jake, Dad, Janette, Leanne,

Mike, Erin, Lauren, Jean, and Denny.

CHAPTER 1

Becca leaned against the cold brick wall with her arms crossed, staring intently out the window of her small office. Her back was to Agent Brach as she watched the leaves dance in the cool autumn breeze blowing through the courtyard of the complex.

It was one of the largest government operated research facilities in the States and strategically situated in an unassuming industrial park near the Hanover Municipal Airport. Its stark appearance from the outside resembled the neighboring warehouses. Once inside, the maze of halls, uniformed military personnel and state-of-the-art security made it feel more like a prison. Becca didn't much care for being so tightly monitored but accepted the security as an inconvenient part of working for the Agency.

She was frustrated with the direction the conversation was going and knew no matter how much she argued with Agent Brach, she wasn't going to win this battle. Becca was young, and a civilian and the older military personnel in the complex treated her as such. She sighed and slowly turned to look at Agent Brach directly. "I'm not comfortable traveling as if I were a captive."

Agent Brach stood his ground and spoke with more authority in his voice than she had detected in the past. "We've done our due diligence and the Agency is not willing to send you to Russia without protection. You stay, or you go with an Agent, it's your choice, Doc." Confident he made his point, he waited for her answer.

Becca ran her fingers through her long dark hair as she contemplated her response. "Fine. I'll be ready at eight o'clock tomorrow morning. Have the agent pick me up at my house. I take it he's been fully briefed and it won't be my responsibility to be his tour guide?"

"Agent Lyndon is fully briefed and understands the delicacy of our relationship with the Russian Government; he'll see you at eight o'clock sharp." Agent Brach nodded his head as if to show his satisfaction with Becca's response and swiftly walked out of her office.

Becca sat down at her desk sinking deep into her leather chair. She picked up the photo of her with her father, knowing if he were there he would agree with the Agency and demand she be well protected. "I know, Dad," she said looking at the photo, "I know."

She reached for her phone and as she entered Agent Lyndon's name next to her eight o'clock departure time she paused, wondering what people would say of her traveling with a man twice her age. All the agents she knew were much older and she fully expected the stares from the younger men wondering if she was traveling with her father, or her much older husband.

Spending most of her life in the lab she had little time to socialize, much less have a relationship of any kind. With a heavy sigh she tossed her phone on the desk and sat back in her chair wishing people would treat her with the same respect they had shown her father.

Becca's father spent the better part of his life in a fortress much the same as the one she now worked in. His advances in genetic alteration were revolutionary and for that reason his work had been closely guarded.

Becca followed in his footsteps, finishing high school early and college in less than three years. After getting her Ph.D. she worked side-by-side with her father, moving to the new Agency complex just six months later. With intimate knowledge of her father's work, it made sense that she would take over his research when he died of heart failure just a year earlier.

Becca's father was completely committed to her, raising her alone since she was just a toddler. Her mother had battled chronic depression and found it impossible to deal with the stress of being married to someone she rarely saw and knew little about. Living in secrecy and spending most of her time alone took its toll on Becca's mother, and when she could no longer function in the isolation, she tucked Becca in her bed and slowly closed the bedroom door, blowing her a kiss before disappearing down the hall.

Becca's father arrived home late that night, as he did most nights, to find the empty pill bottle on the bed next his wife. A note lying on his pillow shared her deepest emotions, her inner demons, and her inability to continue the life she referred to as an emotional and physical prison. Her final words expressed how sorry she was to leave him alone to raise their daughter.

From that moment he knew things had to be different. He didn't want Becca to feel the same pain and isolation and it didn't matter what the Agency had to say. He would only continue his work if Becca was allowed to be with him, whenever, wherever, with no restrictions.

When Becca was old enough to understand the need for secrecy, her father made it a point to share everything about his lifetime of work and involved

Becca in as much as he could. He would take her to the lab and have her clean the test tubes and slides while he worked. Becca practically grew up in the lab, but as long as she could be with her father, she didn't mind where they were.

As the years went by and her passion for science grew, Becca knew exactly what she wanted; she was going to be a scientist, just like her father.

She didn't realize the isolation she would feel, it was new to her. All these years she had her father, and now she was alone. She was hoping this trip to Russia would allow her time to interact with people her own age, outside of the Agency. Agent Brach took that away from her and Agent Lyndon was going to be her chaperone for the next week leaving her little opportunity to shed the overbearing watchful eye of the Agency.

Becca was struggling with her oversized suitcase when she heard the car. She pulled back the curtains and just as she expected, the man walking up the driveway was an older, stuffy looking agent in a black suit, white shirt and black tie. "How typical, another Agent Brach. This should be fun." She said to herself as she watched him walk to the door, opening it before he had a chance to ring the bell.

"Good morning Doctor, looks like a good day for a trip," he said as he reached for her suitcase. "Any other bags to go?"

"No, that's it, thank you," she replied thinking at least he will make himself useful carrying her bags for the next week. She took one last look around the house making sure not to forget anything, grabbed her laptop bag and purse, and followed him to the car.

"Agent Lyndon, I understand you are fully briefed on our trip, I just want to make sure you understand this isn't a..." Becca didn't finish the sentence as she heard a voice respond from behind the open trunk. A bit stunned, she looked at the driver and then back at the trunk lid.

"Yep, briefed and ready for duty," the voice responded from behind the car.

Out of curiosity, Becca walked to the end of the car, but could only see the back of Agent Lyndon as he leaned over to set her bag in the trunk.

He stood up and pointed to the laptop bag in Becca's hand. "Want that bag in the trunk?"

Not many people surprise Becca, but he certainly did. He was not old, not gray, not stuffy looking at all. His white t-shirt and black leather jacket accented his bold and strong physique. His jeans were faded perfectly and long enough to show just the tips of the cowboy boots he was wearing. His dark hair was slightly messy as if he had just run his fingers through it. His reflective glasses didn't allow her to see his eyes, but if they were anything like the chiseled jaw and perfect smile, it would make him the best looking Agent she had seen.

"Uhhhh." The words were flying through her head, but not making it out of her mouth. She finally managed a response. "No, I'll keep it with me, thank you." Her head was tilted to the side making her look as confused as she was.

"Not what you were expecting?" Agent Lyndon asked, knowing exactly what Becca was thinking.

"Not exactly."

Smiling, he shut the trunk. "Good, then let's go."

Becca, caught completely off guard, walked to the open door and sat down in the back seat. As the driver shut the door behind her, the passenger door opened and Agent Lyndon hopped in next to her.

"Isn't what?" he asked.

Becca was confused. "I'm sorry, what?"

"You walked to the car wanting to make sure I understood this trip isn't a..., but you never finished."

"I was going to say this isn't some action packed dangerous mission, but assume a rather boring research trip for an agent."

"Boring research trip and flying to Russia are not really synonymous with each other," he said taking off his sunglasses and slipping them in the pocket of his leather jacket.

Becca was digging through her bag for the itinerary she had printed. She looked up at Agent Lyndon as she handed him the paper. He was smiling and this time she could see his eyes. They did match the rest of him, and he was looking at her as if he could see right through her. Again, she was at a loss for words. As much as she was thrilled not to have an older agent with her, she was absolutely taken off guard by his incredible good looks and obvious confidence. A small scar above his left eye was the only flaw Becca could see in his perfect appearance.

"What's this?" he said, holding his stare at Becca.

"It's our itinerary outlining where we need to be each day."

Agent Lyndon didn't look at the itinerary, instead, handed it back to Becca.

"Aren't you going to look at it?" Feeling somewhat insulted he would not even take the time to look at it, she grabbed the paper and slid it back in her bag.

"You seem a bit, I don't know ... flustered," Agent Lyndon said, laying his head on the back of the seat as if he were getting ready to take a nap.

"It's just that you're not what I expected. I mean, well, you don't look like an agent."

Agent Lyndon closed his eyes. "Well, it seems the Agency wanted someone that was a better fit to travel with you."

"What is that supposed to mean?" Becca responded with a gritty edge.

"Not sure Doc, but the Agency has their reasons." He kept his eyes closed giving her the hint he didn't intend on continuing the conversation.

Becca stewed the rest of the drive to the airport. She was angry Agent Lyndon didn't review the itinerary and frustrated with his comment about being better fit to travel with her. As much as she wanted to grill him, she decided letting him sleep would give her time to regroup. She was a bit embarrassed at her reaction and needed to pull her thoughts together.

She was curious why Agent Lyndon was selected and wondered if it was because she argued not to have an agent at all. He didn't look like an agent, he was younger than the other agents she knew and she had never seen an agent in anything but a suit or uniform. She wondered if he was new, if he had any Agency experience at all, or if he was sent to give the appearance of protection. Either way, it really didn't matter, she had to focus on the reason she was taking this trip.

Meeting with Dr. Levin was critical to the genetic research Becca's father had dedicated his life to. Her father consulted with Dr. Levin during the development stages and his expertise was vital to the successful outcome of the testing. Code-named the Gen-E Project, the highly secretive and controversial genetic alteration process was expected to revolutionize genetic research and the world's approach to cell regeneration. Becca was hoping Dr. Levin would be able to review her research and work through the one obstacle she had consistently experienced.

If she and Dr. Levin could show the results she expected, it would be the culmination of her father's lifetime of work. She wanted more than anything to prove to the scientific community that her father was right, that he had broken through the genetic barrier others could not.

CHAPTER 2

AS THE CAR PULLED UP to the terminal Becca looked over at Agent Lyndon but didn't bother to wake him up. She got out of the car and slammed the door. He slowly stepped out and made his way to the trunk to grab his bag.

Agent Lyndon rubbed his eyes and squinted in the bright sun. "That was quick."

"Usually is when you're sleeping," Becca said as she struggled to get her bag up the curb.

He yawned and stretched. "I didn't get much sleep last night."

"Out too late, Agent Lyndon?" Becca responded with sarcasm in her voice. Not waiting to hear his response, she walked toward the airport entrance towing her oversized bag in one hand, her computer and purse in the other.

He ran after her. "Doc, Doc, hang on a second, where are you going?"

Becca looked up and pointed to the airline sign as if to remind him which airline they were flying and then continued walking toward the door.

Agent Lyndon grabbed her suitcase and turned toward the other end of the arrival gate doors. "Change of plans."

"What change of plans? My itinerary clearly outlines our plans."

Agent Lyndon paused and slowly turned to Becca. "Are you referring to the piece of paper you handed me in the car? I didn't read it because it's not our itinerary."

He got very close to Becca, leaving only a few inches between them, and quietly, but emphatically spoke. "You're working on a top secret project, following in the controversial footsteps of your father, collaborating with a Russian scientist who has spent the better part of his life in prison, and you think traveling on a commercial airline to Russia isn't an issue?"

Becca was completely taken aback by the fact that Agent Lyndon actually knew why he was there, and even more flustered that he had gotten so close to her. "I, I, I didn't …"

"You didn't what, Doc?"

Becca just stood there staring at him, not knowing what to say next.

"Now I know why the Agency assigned me," he said with a bit of frustration in his voice.

"Please do share," she quickly responded.

"As smart as you are, you are completely and utterly lacking common sense, you know, street smarts, and obviously unaware of your situation." Agent Lyndon continued his swift walk toward the private plane boarding area.

Becca followed in silence taking a moment to gather her thoughts. What situation was she in? Based on his tone of voice and direct approach, she thought it would be best to do what he says, at least for now.

"Right on time, Lyndo," the pilot shook Agent Lyndon's hand as they boarded the small jet then turned to greet Becca. "Hello Doctor, welcome aboard. We should be on time and the weather looks good all the way to Moscow."

Becca politely smiled at the pilot and took her seat.

"Thanks Phil, let me know if anything changes." Agent Lyndon sat down in the seat directly across from Becca, setting his leather jacket on the open seat next to him. "Fasten your seatbelt, Doc."

"Lyndo?" Becca asked, curious about his nickname.

"Phil and I have worked together for a long time, I won't fly without him."

Becca fastened her seat belt and looked out the window at the larger commercial planes wondering how she ended up here, on this small jet with Agent Lyndon. Did her sheltered, highly monitored life truly give her a false sense of security? Was the world outside the walls of the Agency that dangerous? If they were, she felt an odd sense of relief that Agent Lyndon was there. She couldn't put her finger on why, especially since all he had done so far is irritate her, but she felt safe with him.

"We're cleared for takeoff," Phil announced over the plane's intercom.

It was better than any commercial flight Becca had ever taken; leather seats, mahogany tables, a small galley in the back, two TVs and a large electronic cluster up front.

"Is this an Agency plane?" Becca wondered why such an expensive plane belonged to an Agency that always told her father they were not a bank and that funding was limited.

"It is, and it isn't," Agent Lyndon responded.

"Can't be both," Becca snapped back as she reached for her laptop.

"You should wait until we are at cruising altitude to work, the ascent can be a bit rough at times in these small jets." Agent Lyndon leaned over and reached in his bag, pulling out a bottle of aspirin.

"Hangover?" Becca asked with a bit of tone, assuming after his nap, and now the aspirin, that he was out late last night.

Agent Lyndon looked at Becca with frustration in his eyes and with a tone closely resembling a parent scolding a child, he offered her a few answers. "No, I was not out late, and no, I don't have a hangover. I spent most of the night making sure you would be able to travel to Russia safely, and more importantly, return safely. The aspirin is for a shoulder injury that bothers me when it's damp and cold, and it's both right now in Russia. But I'm sure you already knew the weather and included it on your itinerary."

She was surprised at his condescending tone. "Now wait a minute, you have no right to talk to me like that. This is my trip, you are here to... well, do whatever it is you do. I told Agent Brach I didn't need protection. This is a research trip not a military exercise." Becca paused for a moment. "What exactly is it that you do and why did they select you?"

He laughed. "I must have drawn the short straw."

"Really, the short straw? That's how the Agency assigns duties now? Glad to see my tax dollars working on Agency strategy." Becca slipped off her shoes and got a little more comfortable in the leather seat. She gazed out the window as the jet took off and the white puffy clouds slowly began to hide the ground below.

Becca didn't know it, but he was staring at her. He was studying her face and recognized the familiar features. She looked just like her father.

Agent Lyndon met Becca's father after graduating from the Academy at the top of his class. He was assigned to shadow the agents protecting her father, and at the time, he thought it was an assignment that completely lacked any kind of challenge. What Agent Lyndon didn't realize was how far the assignment would test his skills, how much it would change his life, and how important a role he would play.

Becca turned from the window to see Agent Lyndon standing next to her with two bottles of water. He opened one and handed it to Becca. "Doc, you and I need to have a talk."

He knew Becca needed protection and felt that sharing his history on the Project would open her eyes to the potential danger she was in. She was stubborn, just like her father, but Agent Lyndon wasn't going to let that get in the way. He needed to make sure she trusted him and the only way to do that was to tell her the truth.

"Not really big on the whole Doc thing, I prefer Becca," she said as she sipped the bottle of water.

"And I prefer Jack," he said taking the seat across from Becca. "I didn't draw the short straw, in fact, sending me was the best option." Jack propped his feet up on the small table that separated the two of them and began to explain.

Becca was not interested in his gloating and assuming he was about to share all the reasons he was a great agent, she turned her attention back to the window, watching the clouds pass by below.

"My first day with the Agency wasn't what I expected..." his voice began to fade. Becca was only half listening as he walked through his first assignment.

"I was hoping for something in the field with a little action; instead, I was put in the Asset Protection division. It wouldn't have been my first choice, but when you get through training they don't really give you a choice. Moving from California to the East Coast was not what I wanted either, hell I didn't even own a winter coat, and it gets way too cold for me in Richmond."

Jack figured Becca wasn't interested in his lack of weather preference, but knew he was about to get her full attention. "Most first days at the Agency are pretty uneventful, not the case for me, my initiation day came with a bit of surprise." He paused long enough for Becca to realize he had stopped talking. He wanted to make sure she was listening. "Did you know fire extinguishers usually work best when pointed directly at the fire?"

Becca turned slowly to look at Jack, her mouth slightly open, her eyes a bit wider than before as the image ran through her mind. "That was you?"

Jack sat there for a moment, happy to see he had her attention, and ever so slightly enjoying the hint of embarrassment he could see on Becca's face. He watched as her cheeks turned a light shade of pink, and found himself admiring the way the natural light shining through the plane window was reflecting in her eyes.

"If you could have seen my hospital room; there I was, comfortably watching the football game while the nurse changed my bandage, and she was .... well, let's just say, not your typical nurse."

Becca rolled her eyes, fully understanding what Jack meant and thinking she must have been beautiful or he would not have even mentioned her.

"Sharpe and ZMan walked in and spoiled a perfectly peaceful afternoon. They had a present for me," he said with a hint of sarcasm, "they gave me a pink container of powder, you know the kind, the same as your grandma had sitting on the sink in her bathroom with the big powder puff." He held his hands out to make a circle, slightly exaggerating the size of the powder puff.

Becca burst out laughing as she pictured this tough, and somewhat overconfident, Agent sitting in a hospital room at the mercy of two Agents and a container of face powder.

"Yep, every birthday I make a trip to the local nursing home with about a dozen of those containers. I find them in my car, at my desk, in my locker at the gym; these guys will never let that go."

"Sorry about the eye," Becca said looking at the scar above his left eye, knowing the one imperfection she found was her fault.

"It's no big deal; I use the powder to cover it up." Jack reached up and touched the scar.

Becca smiled. "I can't believe that was you."

"What were you doing anyway?" Jack asked.

Looking down at her hands, Becca nervously pushed the bracelet on her wrist around and around as she began to tell the story. "It was my first year at the new lab, I was still getting to know my way around; my father was in the middle of running a test when Agent Brach called him out of the lab. He asked me to make sure the burners didn't go out and to watch that the temperature didn't get too high. I walked into the cooling room for just a second, and when I came back, the entire lab table was burning. If I had known how flammable the mixture was I would have never left it alone. I grabbed the fire extinguisher and was close to putting out the fire when you came bursting through the door," she paused and looked up at Jack. "You scared me."

"I must have scared you with the way you whipped around, fire extinguisher in hand."

"I never saw you; I mean I never saw your face, just the blood dripping from the cut above your eye down the side of your completely white face. It did kind of look like you used your grandma's powder."

"I bet it did. I'm just glad I shut my eyes before you blasted me and then smacked me in the head with the fire extinguisher."

"I am truly sorry, Jack," Becca said with sincerity.

"No harm done."

The tension had been broken. Becca was a bit more relaxed as she thought back to that day in the lab; still in disbelief that it was Jack she had hit with the fire extinguisher.

Phil's voice broke the silence. "Hey Lyndo, we're approaching a small disturbance, may want to sit down and buckle up and I'll let you know when we're through."

Becca stood up to reach for her bag. "I just need to grab my notebook."

The plane shook, then dropped. Becca screamed as she fell backward toward the window. Jack quickly grabbed her, his arms held her tight as the plane bounced around like a toy boat in the ocean. "It will be over soon," he said seeing the fear in her eyes.

The sound of Jack's voice was soft and reassuring and the feeling of his strong arms around her gave her a sense of security.

"Thanks, Jack," she said as she glanced up to catch him staring at her. She wasn't sure if the feeling in the pit of her stomach was butterflies from having him hold her or the turbulence. Either way, she felt comfort in his arms.

Phil's voice came back over the speakers. "We should be good to go now, sorry for the short roller coaster ride."

Jack wasn't sorry; he was feeling a connection with Becca and holding her, keeping her safe, was no longer just a job. He felt something, something he had never felt before. His connection with Becca was more than a story about a fire extinguisher, more than the history he had with her father, and more than just another assignment. He was starting to think that fate may have something to do with why he was on this plane, at this time, with her. His protective instincts were overly strong and he knew he would never let anything, or anyone, hurt Becca.

Feeling a bit awkward she stood up and looked down at Jack. "That was a bit scary."

"Normal for a small jet like this," he said thinking it would have been fine if the turbulence had continued giving him an excuse to hold her a bit longer.

"Hungry?" Jack asked.

"I am, actually." Becca sat back in her seat and looked out the window. "It's so beautiful out there, the sky is so blue and the clouds are so peaceful looking."

"At this altitude everything looks a little clearer." Jack was thinking more of what was going on inside the plane than outside.

Becca could still feel exactly where Jack's hands were holding her and could smell his cologne on her shirt. It had been a long time since she was that close to a man. She smiled and ran her hand across the shoulder Jack had just been holding, hoping there would be another time she would feel his strong arms around her.

Jack set down a cup of coffee and bagel on the table in front of Becca. "Black, two sugars, right?"

"How could you possibly know that?"

"It's my job," he said with a coy smile as he sat down with his coffee in one hand and a donut in the other.

He watched Becca as she paged through the research results she would be sharing with Dr. Levin and could see the puzzled look on her face as she studied one page longer than the others. "You look confused," he said.

"It's just that the test results on this page are an anomaly, they aren't consistent with the rest of the results. I am really hoping Dr. Levin can offer some clarity. His knowledge of identifying genetic characteristics is very close to the way my father approached the regeneration spectrum. Other than my father, he is one of the few doctors in the world with the knowledge and experience to understand this type of data." Becca reached down to grab her coffee when she realized Jack was just sitting there, staring at her. "I'm sorry, this is probably incredibly boring to you, there's not a lot of action in genetic research."

"Actually, I'm a lot closer to it than you know."

Becca sipped her coffee, waiting for Jack to explain.

"Do you believe in fate, Becca?"

She wondered why Jack would ask her a question like that. "Never really thought about it, my brain thinks more in black and white." Setting down her coffee, she watched as Jack touched the scar above his eye and it suddenly clicked. "What were you doing at the lab that day?" she asked.

"Asset protection," Jack responded avoiding eye contact with Becca. He knew what he was about to share would change her entire perspective. "Becca, my asset was your father."

Becca looked blankly at Jack as her eyes welled up with tears. "You knew my father?"

"I did, very well," he paused for a moment, "you look just like him, Becca." Jack leaned over and handed Becca a tissue. "Your father dedicated his life to this research and he would be very proud knowing you are continuing his work. He was getting very close to finding her, to finding Gen-E."

Becca listened as Jack walked through the five years he was assigned to protect her father, sounding more like a debrief report than sentiment. She started to question the chemistry she thought they had, wondering if this assignment was just another part of the job.

He paced back and forth telling Becca about the many research trips. He knew so much about her father, about her, and yet, she knew nothing about him.

"I ... I don't understand how it's possible that I never saw you except for the lab that day."

"Part of asset protection is being invisible to potential threats, and the only way to remain completely undetected is to make sure no one knows who you are protecting, or why. Not even the people closest to the asset."

Irritated, Becca snapped at Jack. "Can you stop calling my father an asset?"

"Sorry, Becca, just part of the job, never identify an asset by name. It ensures their anonymity, and because it's less personal, it keeps the agent focused on the job and keeps the emotion out of it." Jack was talking the talk of a true agent, not realizing how hard it was for Becca to hear.

"Were you there that day? Were you with my father when he died?"

Jack knew no good would come from telling her the truth; it wouldn't bring her father back. Jack wasn't there when it happened, and often wondered if things may have been different if he had been. "I was in a base hospital recovering from an emergency appendectomy; it took me out of commission for a week. After your father passed I was reassigned to asset recovery with Sharpe and ZMan."

Becca wiped her eyes with the tissue. "So Jack, am I just another asset?"

"There was no short straw Becca, you need to know that I asked for this assignment. It's important to me to do whatever I can to help you find Gen-E, to help you finish the work your father dedicated his life to."

Jack reached out to gently grasp her hands in his. "Becca, I promised your father if anything ever happened I would make sure you were safe. And although the Agency thinks I am too close to this to be effective, I argued I was the only one qualified for the assignment."

All Becca could do was look at Jack and nod her head in agreement. The emotions were so strong and for someone like Becca, it was unchartered territory. Her attraction to Jack was real, that much she knew, but finding out he had been part of her life for years was confusing. She sat there quietly for what seemed to be an eternity trying to make sense of everything she had just heard. Maybe Jack was right, maybe, just maybe, fate was part of the equation.

If Becca was anything like her father, Jack knew he needed to let her process the information he had shared. He gave her the time she needed and watched her as she stared out the window resting her chin on her hand. He had seen that look before; it was exactly what her father would do when he was deep in thought.

Looking at his watch, Jack walked to the cabinet in the back of the plane and pulled out a silver case. He set it down on the table in front of Becca and clicked it open. It was time to give Becca a dose of reality. She needed to understand the potential danger she was in and why he was there.

"What's that?" Becca asked as she turned her attention from the view outside the plane to Jack.

"It's time for us to go over a few things."

She watched as Jack pulled out a large file, photos and a map. "You must take your job pretty seriously Jack. Is asset protection really that involved?"

"You don't get it do you, Becca? Your father did a great job of protecting you from the ugly side of his research. But now you need to understand what's at stake."

Jack held up a photo. "You know this guy?" Before Becca could respond, he held up a second picture. "How about this one?"

"Never saw either of them in my life," Becca answered.

He sifted through the photos and paused, looking at one a little longer than the rest. He slowly pulled it out of the stack and handed it to Becca. "This is why I am here."

Becca took the photo from Jack, looking first at him, then down at the photo. "Where did you get this, I don't understand." There was a hint of fear in her voice. "Did you take this?" She stared at the photo of her with her father in New York, just days before he died.

Jack held up a photo of a man with long slicked back hair and eyes that were as black as night. "He did."

"Jack, you're scaring me. Who is that?" Becca pulled her legs up on the seat and wrapped her arms around her knees.

"The picture of you and your father in New York was taken by Maxim Binovich, one nasty Russian; he works for the Russian underground that has been trying to acquire Gen-E from your father."

"Is that why we had to leave New York early?"

"Binovich got too close and the Agency demanded that you and your father return to

THE GEN-E PROJECT • 28

Richmond. Although he got too close, it was a break we had been waiting for. Until then we thought it was the Russian Mob looking to get their hands on Gen-E. After seeing Binovich, the Agency intercepted a message he sent with that picture of you and your father and followed the links straight back to the Russian underground, run by this guy," Jack held up another photo, "Adrian Nilov; and knowing what I know about Nilov, it would have been better if it was the Mob. At least the Mob is predictable and monitored by the International Organized Crime Division. The Agency hasn't been able to hang on to any trail of Nilov for longer than a week or two, and he knows it."

"Jack, they know who I am," Becca said with fear in her voice.

"They do know who you are Becca, but they didn't know you were continuing the work on Gen-E until you called Dr. Levin asking for his help. The Agency monitors Dr. Levin hoping to get close to Nilov and finally put him behind bars. When you called Dr. Levin the Agency discovered they weren't the only ones listening; Nilov intercepted the call and knows how close you are to finding Gen-E."

Becca sat back in her seat, wondering how this could be happening. It was too much information for her analytical brain to comprehend. One thing she was certain of; the Agency knew about Nilov before they left for Russia. "Why didn't anyone tell me, Jack? Why did the Agency let me leave? Why are we on this plane to Russia?" Becca fired off one question after the other, leaving Jack no time to respond.

"Take a deep breath, Becca. We couldn't tell you, we needed you to believe you were following the itinerary you created. As far as letting you go to Russia, you know the Agency has committed as much time and resources to the Gen-E Project as both you and your father have, so they are counting on Dr. Levin's help and a positive outcome."

"Jack, am I being used as bait?"

"No, Becca, you're not. The Agency would never put you in that position, and if you were, they would have let you fly commercial, had agents all over that plane and at every stop on your itinerary, and you would have never known. This is a well-orchestrated visit with Dr. Levin, after which we are back on this plane and headed home."

Becca understood now why she and her father rarely traveled, and why when they did, they always deviated from the planned itinerary. It was the Agency's way of keeping her and her father safe, but the New York trip was different. The itinerary said they were going to visit the Statue of Liberty on Tuesday and Becca begged her father not to change it. That one time he gave in, he stuck to the schedule and Binovich found them.

As much as Becca hated the reason she was holding that picture, she cherished it at the same time; it was the last picture of her and her father together before he died.

Becca knew the research was far more advanced than anyone else in the world was working on and that the Gen-E Project was closely guarded. The liability was always in the back of her mind, but the way her father lived his life guarded her from the dangers that faced her now.

The Agency security she had so easily dismissed was now the one thing that would keep Nilov from getting his hands on Gen-E.

"What now, Jack?" Becca was in unchartered territory, she was no longer in control and more than anything, she was afraid.

Over the next few hours Jack walked through every step of their time in Russia. Becca listened as he explained everything, waiting for her to absorb each step before moving on. She now understood why he was so tired, the next few days were so meticulously planned he must have worked on it nonstop for weeks. Listening to each detail, she knew he was committed to protecting her, and as scared as she was, she was glad it was Jack at her side.

Phil passed through the cabin to grab a bottle of water. "Lyndo, we're sixty minutes from Moscow," he said as he looked at Becca seeing a hint of fear in her eyes. "You've got Lyndo, you'll be just fine, Doc." Phil's voice was comforting and confident; he smiled at Becca as he walked back to the cockpit and closed the door behind him.

Jack walked over to the tall line of cabinets in the front of the plane and pulled out two garment bags and a suitcase. "We are arriving as Mr. and Mrs. Barnes, antiquity dealers there to evaluate an art collection for our client in the States." He tossed Becca her new passport. "Since they know who you are we need to change the way you look."

Jack handed her one of the garment bags. "You can change in the back, the curtain draws closed to give you some privacy. Oh, and this is for your computer and research."   He set a new briefcase down on the seat.

The clothes were designer and very expensive, and the briefcase was something Becca would never have the money to buy herself.

Becca changed and opened the curtain. Looking stunning and very refined, Jack couldn't help but stare. She smoothed out the few wrinkles on the sleeves. "It fits, but somehow I think you knew that already."

"It most certainly does," Jack agreed as he handed her a wig and contact case. "You will need these too."

"Really, Jack, is this necessary?"

"It is, look at your passport photo." Jack walked to the back and closed the curtain.

She looked down at the passport and in an instant she was no longer Becca. As she glanced at her reflection in the mirror, adjusting the wig to fit just right, her thoughts were racing trying to figure out how she left this morning as Becca, a brunette with brown eyes, and now stood in this small jet halfway around the world, as the blond, green-eyed antiquities dealer, Mrs. Barnes, married to the fictitious Mr. Barnes.

"Jack, are you wearing a disguise too?" Becca turned to see Jack as he opened the curtain.

"Well, I guess you'll do as Mr. Barnes." She gazed at Jack, thinking it was impossible for him to look any better than he did in jeans and a leather jacket, but this was better, much better. An expensive suit and silk tie fit him well. "No wig for you?"

"They haven't seen me before, and I don't make a good blond." He smiled at Becca as he handed her a small box.

"What's this?"

"Well, to be Mrs. Barnes you need a ring."

It was by far the biggest diamond she had ever seen, surrounded by little Princess cut diamonds, too many to count.

"I always imagined the day I would get married, but never quite pictured it like this." Becca slipped the ring on her finger knowing it would be a perfect fit. "It's beautiful, Jack. What if I lose it?"

"Not an option, unless you want to owe the Agency half a million dollars."

"What? This is real?"

"Can't pose as high-end antiquity dealers with a fake, now can we? Nilov knows you are arriving today and he'll have all the inbound traffic monitored. We need to play the part to ensure his focus is elsewhere."

"Jack, Dr. Levin is expecting to meet with me the day after tomorrow. What will happen if I don't show up? Is he in any danger because of me?"

"Dr. Levin is well guarded by the Russian government; it would be difficult for Nilov to get close to him. All their attention is focused on you right now; they expect you to be an easier target."

"What happens when they realize I'm not on the commercial flight?"

"You are on that plane, at least that's what Nilov will think. Agent Branson is on that plane, in your seat right now. It was too dangerous for us to allow you to go see Dr. Levin, and since they don't let him out of the lab unescorted, the Agency has made arrangements with the Russian Government to bring Levin to us. Agent Branson will travel disguised as you to the Russian Lab to meet with Dr. Levin. Nilov knows getting to you on the way to the lab is his best chance of securing Gen-E. If Nilov takes the bait, it will buy us enough time for you to meet with Dr. Levin and give the Agency the chance to finally bring down Nilov."

Becca watched as Jack slipped on an expensive watch and could see his frustration as he fumbled with the clasp. She took his hand, turning it so she could see the clasp. Gently folding the clasp closed she held his hand a bit longer than she needed to. His hands were strong and touching him gave her the same feeling she had when he held her earlier during the turbulence. She looked up, close enough to feel his breath on her cheek. He put his hands on her arms and held her tight as the plane turned toward the Moscow airport.

"I think it's best if we take our seats for the rest of the flight," Jack said as he guided Becca back to her seat.

CHAPTER 3

It was a long time ago when Dr. Levin became a ward of the Russian Government. He was well respected in the scientific community and gave Russia hopes of moving to the forefront of genetic research. His work, although similar to Becca's father, was focused on brain activity and the link between genetics and human intelligence.

Dr. Levin belonged to an elite group of Russian scientists who lived and worked within the heavily guarded Penza Institute, just south of Moscow, and his future was on a path worthy of Nobel consideration. With his status and limited accessibility, Dr. Levin's circle of associates was limited to a small research team, a handful of other elite scientists, high-ranking military personnel, and politicians who used the Penza Institute successes as leverage for personal gain.

Life at the Penza Institute took its toll on Dr. Levin. He cherished the few days each month he was able to spend with his wife even though leaving the Institute meant he was under the watchful eyes of a Penza security team. The stifling lifestyle was affecting his work and he was not shy about voicing his discontent with the increasing demands on his team and limited contact with the outside world.

When approached by the Russian Justice Minister with a promise of more freedom and the ability to work in a lab closer to his wife, Dr. Levin could not refuse. Blinded by the hope of more freedom, Dr. Levin agreed to help the Minister. It would be a decision he would regret the rest of his life.

At the time the Minister approached him, Dr. Levin believed he was giving the Minister's wife the chance to die peacefully, without the pain of a long drawn out battle that would inevitably end in death. For his freedom, Dr. Levin agreed to assist in ending the Minister's wife's fight with cancer. Though she died peacefully in her husband's arms, the news of what Dr. Levin had done created a public outcry for justice and both the Minister and Dr. Levin were tried and convicted of murder.

Losing his research was heartbreaking, but tolerable compared to the pain Dr. Levin would endure when his wife turned her back on him. She left shortly after the trial. Unable to face the public scrutiny of her husband's actions, he would learn a year later that she succumbed to the relentless badgering and embarrassment, taking her own life while living with her parents in eastern Russia.

The news devastated Dr. Levin and he believed with his whole heart that his wife suffered the same consequences as those he had inflicted on the Minister's wife.

Serving his life sentence in a Russian prison was no different than the life he had led inside the Institute and now without his wife, he didn't care if he ever left the small eight-foot cell. The Russian Government reached out to Dr. Levin throughout the years offering him a lab in the prison and the opportunity to secretly continue his work; he adamantly refused every time. The agony over his actions and the death of his wife fueled his hatred of the Government. He vowed he would never provide his assistance again.

It wasn't until he was approached by Becca's father that he would consider research again. The Russian Government had tried many times to sway his decision and only allowed him to work with Becca's father in hopes it would get Dr. Levin back into the lab.

Dr. Levin felt a connection to Becca's father knowing both their wives had met the same fate and over the years they forged a close friendship. He felt compelled to offer his expertise and supported Becca's father in the development of the Gen-E Project. His work on the Project rekindled his passion for genetic research and he reluctantly agreed to again support the efforts of the Russian Government.

Dr. Levin's early release from prison was kept highly secretive and he was relocated to a lab in Kazan, Russia, to continue his work where he would remain heavily guarded. Access to the outside world was non-existent for Dr. Levin; the lab was a fortress and completely cut-off from life beyond the tall concrete walls.

Working with the younger scientists was frustrating for Dr. Levin, his passion and deep commitment to genetic research was no match for the next generation. His frustration with their lack of conviction was deepened when he discovered his assistant had smuggled in a cell phone and was looking at the online hockey scores. Dr. Levin knew if the guards discovered the phone he would need to train a new assistant. He took the phone, promising to return it at the end of the day as long as the young man never brought it back to the lab again.

Sitting in his office, Dr. Levin took the phone out of his pocket and set it on his desk. Although he would never openly admit it, he was enamored by the power of these devices and knew that access to the outside world was now in his hands.

Looking around the lab through the glass windows of his office he made sure the guards could not see him. He picked up the phone and searched for his wife's name and home-town hoping to find where she had been laid to rest. Reading through the obituary his heart was heavy with sadness. In complete disbelief, he had to read the last sentence three times: "Survived by her daughter, Alena Levinova." His hand covered his mouth to muffle the gasp as he dropped the phone on the desk. It was at that very moment he decided he would do whatever it took to find the daughter he never knew he had.

CHAPTER 4

As THE PLANE LANDED Becca could see the Moscow lights shimmering in the clear night sky. She was afraid of how the next few days would unfold and felt a bit of disappointment knowing she would not be able to see all the things she wanted to. "It looks different than I expected."

"Always does when you know what you're walking into." Jack handed her a beautiful black floor length coat and cashmere scarf. "You're going to need these."

"Enjoy your time in Moscow, Mr. and Mrs. Barnes. I'll see you in a few days," Phil said as Becca and Jack walked down the stairs to the black limo waiting on the tarmac.

"Dobro požalovat'!" The driver said as he opened the limo door.

"Spasibo," Jack confidently replied, thanking the driver.

Becca looked at him, surprised he knew Russian. He gave her a little nod and a slight smile as they got in the car.

Jack was nothing like anyone she had ever met, he was intriguing, intelligent, and confident. She was impressed, and even after a frustrating first day with Jack, she found herself completely captivated by him.

The drive to the hotel was quiet, Jack was clear in his instructions that they speak as little as possible when in the company of anyone they did not know and trust.

As they made their way through the city the sun was beginning to rise showing just a hint of the bold-colored buildings. Becca closed her eyes and pictured how it would have looked if she didn't know what she knew now.

Becca said nothing as they checked in at the hotel and made their way through the beautifully ornate lobby to the elevators. She felt as if everyone was staring at her and wondered if any of them knew who she was, who she really was.

They entered the suite, Jack tipped the bellman and closed and locked the door with the deadbolt. Becca stood in the living room looking out the full wall of windows admiring how beautiful the city looked from the safe confines of the hotel. "Someday," she said, "someday."

"There will be another time; you'll have an opportunity to come back."

"I know, but it just won't look the same. It's different now and no one can change that."

The morning sunlight was shining just enough to highlight Becca's beautiful silhouette. Jack watched as she crossed her arms and gently rubbed her hands along the silk sleeves of her blouse. He knew what she was going through; her world would look different now, no matter where she was. Her innocence was gone, and the way she lived would be very different than what she has known. Her father protected her well and now it was up to Jack to watch over her.

"I can turn up the heat if you're cold," he said as he walked toward the bar. "Maybe a glass of wine?"

"No thank you, Jack, I am too tired for wine. I'm going to take a warm shower."

"I'll be out for a bit, take some time to relax, we have an art collection to view this afternoon."

Becca stopped at the bedroom door and abruptly turned to look at Jack. "What, that's for real? Jack, they'll peg me immediately as a complete novice. A box of crayons and some blank paper is the closest I've ever been to real artwork."

"Where's the faith? Do you think I would let you walk into a situation completely unprepared?"

Jack handed her a portfolio containing photographs and descriptions of all the art pieces they would be seeing later that day.

"Take some time to review the pieces and do your best to memorize the comments in the recap. I've got this, you won't need to talk much, just follow my lead. The sellers have been briefed and were told that Mrs. Barnes is a woman of few words and if I remember correctly, 'completely arrogant' might be somewhere in the bio they were provided." He smiled and walked toward the door.

"Arrogant, really? After taking a few cues from you, I am confident I can pull that off." Becca gave Jack a coy smile.

"While I am gone don't use the phone and don't answer the door for anyone."

He was serious and Becca fully understood.

"I won't Jack, I promise."

Jack took the stairs down to the lobby making sure he knew every option for a quick exit in case they couldn't use the elevators. He made his way through the lobby taking notice of every person. His training served him well and he was able to dismiss each of them as non-threats. He was confident he had meticulously planned this trip to ensure Becca's safety.

Meeting with his Russian contacts, Jack went over the plans making sure to cover every possible obstacle and address each potential gap with contingency plans.

The four men were trusted Agency reps, well trained asset protection and recovery agents stationed in Russia to protect American government officials visiting Moscow. All of them fully expected to have Nilov in custody within 72 hours.

Jack had done his homework and set up the meeting with Dr. Levin at the same time Becca had originally planned. Agent Branson, posing as Becca, would depart Moscow with the other Agents en route to Dr. Levin's research facility while Becca met with the real Dr. Levin just two blocks from the hotel.

Jack fully understood what was at stake; not just Becca's safety and the safety of the other agents, but the Agency's expectation of finding Gen-E.

Jack spent enough time with Becca's father to know Gen-E was revolutionary, and he was fully invested in making sure Becca was given the opportunity to work with Dr. Levin. Jack couldn't impact the outcome of the research, but was committed to making sure Becca and the Doctor would be safe.

Jack left the other agents and drove the perimeter of the abandon building just down the block from the hotel, observing every point of entry and exit and the surrounding buildings. He watched the locals and assessed the roads and traffic patterns, taking note of the businesses on the block that would be open while Becca and the Dr. Levin were inside. Confident that nothing was out of place, Jack was comfortable with the plan and called Ben to give him the green light.

Ben was lead man in Russia and better known as Wheeler for his ability to drive just about anything. His skills on the road were like no one else Jack knew and were often the topic of training room talk back in the States. Jack was confident with the plan and the team that would be with Agent Branson while she traveled to the Russian lab.

Becca was sitting in front of the fireplace studying the artwork when Jack arrived back at the hotel.

"Where did you go Jack?"

"I met with our local team to do a final plan review for our meeting with Dr. Levin and Agent Branson's trip to the Russian lab; everything is a go."

He handed Becca a cup of coffee admiring how beautiful she looked in the warm glow of the fire. Although he thought she was stunning as a blond, the brunette hair hidden beneath the wig was much more fitting of her personality.

"Agent Branson won't be in any danger, right, Jack?"

"She will be just fine, she knows how to take care of herself and she has Wheeler. That guy can drive. If there is any sign of trouble he will make sure she is out of harm's way."

"I hope so, Jack, I hope so."

"Are you ready to go view some art, Mrs. Barnes?"

"As ready as I will ever be. I never studied this hard for final exams in college; I hope I remember what to do so I don't blow our cover."

"I'm sure you will be fine, just follow my lead." Jack held Becca's coat as she slipped it on. He slid his hand down to the small of her back as he guided her toward the door.

Arriving at the museum the chauffeur opened the door for Jack. He walked around the car and held his hand out to assist Becca. The art collector's agent, Benjamin Frederick, was waiting just outside the private museum entrance.

"Good day, Mr. and Mrs. Barnes, I hope your travel to Moscow was uneventful."

"It was, Ben, thank you for asking," Jack responded making direct eye contact with Ben as he walked through the open door.

They entered the private art gallery and were immediately greeted by two security guards. In perfect character, Becca removed her coat and handed it to one of the guards. "Make sure to hang this up, I don't wear wrinkles well," she said, ignoring the stunned look on the guards face.

Ben fumbled his clipboard as he frantically reached for the coat. He whispered his apology to the guard as he took her coat and quickly followed Jack and Becca, stopping briefly to hang it up in the closet.

The afternoon was exhilarating for Becca as she held true to her character, offering only the short one-lined remarks she had read earlier that day. It was apparent that her tone and demeanor were wearing on Ben when he began directing more of his questions toward Jack.

Becca knew what Ben was doing and thought she would live up to her completely arrogant bio. "Tell me, Ben, is this piece one you would place in a foyer or a study?"

Ben's fear of her tone was clear in his shaky response. "Well, Mrs. Barnes, if I were to own a piece of this size with such bold subject matter, I would place it in a study on a wall all its own so as not to detract from its beauty."

"Really? Then you're not as familiar with our buyer as I had hoped because he would certainly place it in the foyer to make sure it was the first piece his guests saw when they entered his home. Do you know why that is, Mr. Frederick?" Becca asked as she turned toward Ben to see his reaction.

Ben stood there searching for the right words, but Becca didn't give him time to answer.

"You see, Ben, our buyer is one that demands respect and a piece such as this makes a statement. It sets a very specific tone and establishes his power from the moment guests arrive in his home."

Jack couldn't help but give Becca a smile in admiration of how perfectly she played Mrs. Barnes.

Feeling bad for Ben, Jack stepped in. "Ben, I believe it's time to move on."

Ben led the way down a corridor, his walk a bit deflated from earlier in the afternoon. Jack glanced over at Becca and gave her a roll of his eyes. She perked her lips and shrugged her shoulders as if to say she was completely happy with her portrayal of Mrs. Barnes.

The corridor led to a large intricately carved wooden door that opened to an oval shaped, dimly lit gallery. In the center of the room, surrounded by red velvet stanchions, was a statue of a woman looking down in admiration at the young girl she was holding in her arms.

The complete silence was broken only by Becca's footsteps on the tile floor echoing in the domed ceiling as she approached the sculpture. This piece was not in the file Jack had given her that morning and she was completely unprepared.

For the first time Becca understood the power of art and the deep-seeded passion that engulfs an individual when explaining how art speaks to the soul. This piece took her breath away and brought her back to the distant memory of her mother. Her eyes were glazed as she brought her arms up and wrapped them around herself as if she was trying to hold her emotions in check.

Jack watched as Becca stood there silently staring at the sculpture. She was oblivious to Ben's background narrative of its origin and to the fact that Jack was staring at her. He was drawn to her emotional reaction and captivated by her vulnerability. As much as Jack wanted to allow Becca time to immerse herself in the moment, it was clear Mrs. Barnes was quickly fading and he had no choice but to bring her back to the reality they were in.

"Darling, I think Ben has set up drinks in the courtyard for us." Jack placed his arm around Becca and walked her out the glass door on the far side of the gallery whispering quietly, "I thought I lost you for a second, Mrs. Barnes."

Becca managed a slight smile and looked over her shoulder at Ben who was quickly tagging behind.

She sat quietly as they sipped champagne and listened to Ben and Jack review the collection. She actually felt a bit bad for Ben knowing that he would never hear from them again and would have to explain to the owner that the potential buyer had lost interest.

It was early evening when the chauffeur picked them up from the museum. Becca listened as Jack and the driver spoke back and forth in Russian. The car stopped and as Jack helped her out she realized they were not at the hotel. He escorted her up the walkway to a glass door under an awning that opened exposing a beautifully decorated foyer.

"Don't know about you, Mrs. Barnes, but I'm starving," Jack said as he led Becca to the bar ordering two glasses of champagne. He handed Becca her glass and held his up to toast, "to you, to me, to Mr. and Mrs. Barnes."

They enjoyed a quiet dinner talking about the art collection and how well Becca had played Mrs. Barnes.

As the evening moved on she wasn't sure if it was the champagne, the lack of sleep, or the long plane ride, but she was feeling a bit foggy. It was difficult for her to concentrate on what Jack was saying. Instead she found herself watching his lips as he spoke and wanting more than anything for him to lean over the table and kiss her. He was so handsome in his suit and his demeanor was captivating. His constant affectionate attention toward her was giving Becca every reason to believe he would kiss her if given the chance.

Jack could sense Becca was not herself. He knew he had put her though a lot in a short time and could tell the few glasses of champagne had gone straight to her head.

After dinner he took the slightly tipsy Becca back to the hotel and let her get the sleep she so desperately needed. He sat in the chair next to the bed admiring how the soft light from the hallway highlighted her face, and how her long dark hair flowed across the pillow.

Becca woke up to the smell of coffee and could tell that she had slept alone in the bed that night.

"Good morning, or should I say, good afternoon?" Jack asked as he glanced at the clock on the wall. "Hope you like coffee in the afternoon."

"I can't believe I slept that long. Coffee sounds perfect." Becca slipped on the hotel bathrobe and sat down at the table. "Did you sleep at all last night?"

"I fell asleep in the chair and have the back ache to prove it. Would you prefer crepes or an omelet?"

Becca reached for the crepes. "What are we doing today, Jack?"

"We are going to sit tight. I've arranged for Dr. Levin to meet us at the lab at five o'clock tomorrow morning when traffic is light and it's easier to spot anything that's out of place."

Becca listened as he continued going over the perfectly laid plan and meticulous timing. She heard every word he said, but her mind wandered, she was looking at Jack in a way she had never looked at a man before. Was it because he was her protector, her guardian, or was it because she truly felt something for him?

Jack was fully aware of the way Becca was looking at him. She was so deep in her thoughts she didn't even realize he had stopped talking.

Jack slowly pushed away from the table and walked over to her chair, her gaze following him the entire way. He took the cup of coffee out of her hand and set it on the table then turned to look at her, his face just inches from hers. He paused only a moment before leaning in and kissing her. She kissed him back with more passion than she knew she had, and it was everything she had hoped it would be.

He caressed her face with his hand as she closed her eyes placing her hand over his. His strong arms lifted her out of the chair and carried her to the bedroom.

CHAPTER 5

WAKING UP NEXT TO JACK was not what Becca had planned, but given the choice she would have stayed there all day. The night before was magical and Becca didn't want the feeling she had at that very moment to end.

Jack brushed the hair away from her eyes. "Morning."

"How long have you been staring at me?"

"You know you talk in your sleep?"

"I know I do, my father always said I would tell stories. What was it about this time? Was I flying a balloon or hiking Mt. Everest?"

"Actually this time you wanted to find the box in the ground. You knew where it was and you were going to dig until you found it."

Becca, a bit embarrassed, tried adding a little humor. "I hope there's treasure in that box."

"Care to share more?"

"Really, it's not a big deal and you'll probably laugh."

"Try me."

"I love to hunt for treasure and when I have time I like to take a walk with my metal detector. It's the thrill you get when you find something and wonder where it came from, whose it was, and how it got there. It's relaxing, yet exciting, and it clears my mind."

"Ever find anything good?"

She was certain Jack would think it was silly, but he seemed genuinely interested. "I've found a couple things. One time I found a necklace from the 18th century, it was in an old tin and wrapped in leather. You could still make out the rough engraving on the back. It's amazing how something that old can be so well preserved."

"Do you keep or sell what the things that you find?"

"I have a special box that belonged to my mother that I keep everything in. The value isn't as important as the story behind the piece."

"I found treasure once," Jack said, "I was down in the Keys a few years back and did some diving. There was this reef that was popular with divers and teeming with fish. Sharpe and I were down for only a few minutes when I spotted a coin that must have been uncovered from the recent storms. I grabbed it and put it in my wetsuit and kept going. We were getting ready to head to the surface when I saw a shadow coming toward the reef, a big shadow. As it got closer I could clearly see it was a shark and he was headed straight for me, passing so close that I could have counted the teeth in his mouth. He circled and came back again, this time passing by Sharpe. We were both floating there not knowing if we should surface or stay put; that shark was big and he looked hungry. Lucky for us he kept going and that was the end of our dive."

"I would have panicked," Becca said. "I am not a fan of the water and adding a shark in the mix would send me right over the edge."

"The water is my solace, like your open field and metal detector. I'll make you a deal, you teach me how to find treasure on the land and I will teach you how to find treasure under the water."

Becca welcomed the invitation, not so much to be in the water, but to know Jack wanted to spend time with her outside of this chaos. The feelings she had for Jack were real and she was getting the impression he felt the same way. "Deal," she said as she rested her head on Jack's chest.

He held her close and kissed the top of her head. "I'd rather stay here all day, but we need to get going. How about I run down to the café and grab us some breakfast?"

Jack walked back in the room, setting the coffee down on the table next to Becca's laptop. He could hear the shower and knew he would have just a small window of opportunity.

He grabbed his bag, quickly connecting the cables to Becca's laptop and clicked on the security password entry box. Jack ran through everything they had talked about, everything she had said trying to pinpoint the words that were important to her and the one word that would unlock her laptop. He typed in her father's name but it didn't work, then he tried JENNY thinking she would have never used GEN-E, but again, it didn't work. He had one chance left before the computer locked which would mean he would have to tell Becca, and she would never trust him again. Jack slowly typed in the only other word that he could possibly think of: TREASURE. The home screen popped up as he heard her turn off the shower.

The data transfer took longer than he had anticipated. He knew he was taking the chance on Becca walking out to see his equipment connected to her computer. He watched as the minutes slowly ticked by and finally the 'transfer finished' message appeared. Jack had just enough time to clear his equipment and set out the to-go containers from the café before Becca walked out of the bedroom.

Becca sat down at the table and Jack reviewed the day ahead while they had breakfast. "You're comfortable with the plan?" Jack asked.

"Absolutely, and looking forward to hearing what Dr. Levin thinks about the new direction I took. He provided a lot of great insight while my father worked on this project and I am really hoping he can confirm what I believe is the final step. If we are able to come away with the final formula, it will literally change the human body's healing capabilities. It will be the biggest scientific breakthrough in recent history."

"Tell me, Becca, how did your father keep all this straight in his head? He never carried a laptop and he didn't have anything on paper. How is it that he never wrote anything down?"

"You know your life, right Jack? I mean, you could tell stories of your life from as far back as you can remember without having to read it off a piece of paper. Right?"

"Yeah, I guess."

"Gen-E was my father's life, he lived it every day and he knew her so well he didn't have to write it down. Not me, I am way too dependent on my laptop and I just don't have what my father had, he was a very special man. I am also at the mercy of the Agency who has to have everything in their control and backed up, and then a back-up of the back-up."

"Your father definitely was a very special man, Becca and you're a lot like your father. Your determination is as strong, if not stronger, than his. He would be proud Becca, very proud."

"Thanks, Jack, but let's not get ahead of ourselves. We still need to get through today."

"Then let's get you started. We don't have much time with Dr. Levin and I want to make sure you have everything you need at the lab before he gets there." Jack held her coat as she stood up and slipped it on.

"Thank you, Mr. Barnes," she said with a smile.

He held the door open for her. "You are most certainly welcome, Mrs. Barnes."

Jack and Becca approached the old concrete building just a few blocks from the hotel. The building looked as if it had been there for a hundred years, and although she could not read the Russian signs, Becca knew the warnings were meant to keep people out. Yellow tape blocked the doorways and every first floor window was boarded.

The dust fell as Jack opened the large steel door. "Jack, is this safe?"

"It is for today." Jack guided Becca down the long hallway and up to the second floor, stopping at a door clearly marked with a hazardous sign. He held it open as Becca walked in the large room.

"Jack, this is incredible. How did you get all this equipment here? How did you know what I needed?" She was amazed at how perfectly the lab was set up and how everything she and Dr. Levin would need was there.

"You have to remember, I did this for your father and he had a very specific list of what he needed." He watched Becca wander through the lab touching everything as if it were Christmas morning.

"It's perfect, Jack, thank you."

"I will be outside if you need me. I'm going to watch for Dr. Levin to arrive. Oh, and by the way, you'll want to watch the cracks in the floor, they go a couple floors down." Jack walked out the door leaving Becca to get comfortable in the lab.

She turned on all the equipment, set up her laptop, and laid her research on the lab table so Dr. Levin could see the progression of the steps she had taken. It was her hope that he would be able to help her identify the obstacle that was holding her back from finding Gen-E.

Feeling both excited and nervous, Becca had an uncomfortable feeling in the pit of her stomach. Her father always taught her to go with her instinct, but until now, she had never felt unsafe. She wondered if Jack was rubbing off on her, or maybe she was being just a bit paranoid. Giving in to the insecure feeling, she reached in her pocket and pulled out her phone. She entered the synch menu and was about to start the synch when she heard a deep, warm voice.

"I'm looking for Becca."

Becca slid the phone back in her pocket and turned around to see the Doctor; he was smiling as he removed his dark hat and top coat.

"Dr. Levin, it is wonderful to see you."

The Doctor held his arms out greeting Becca with a big hug. "I'm so sorry about your father," he said in his thick Russian accent as he stepped back to look at Becca. "You are not the little girl I remember from the pictures your father sent me. You are a beautiful young lady now, and a smart one at that."

"Thank you, Dr. Levin."

The Doctor walked over to the lab table to study her work. He ran his finger from one result to the next, stopping only briefly as he reviewed the changes Becca had made. "This step here, you did this?"

"Yes Doctor, I was consistently getting corrupt results when testing at that step, so I minimized the enzyme mixture to create a continuous path for the antibodies."

"Hmm." Was the only sound Dr. Levin made as he continued to study her work.

It seemed like an eternity as she waited for him to react to what he was seeing.

"You are your father's daughter," he said as he turned to look at Becca, "you've done well; you resolved the breakdown problem he was having. Yes?"

"I have, but I am unable to find the same resolution to the absorption barrier at the final step. I have tried hundreds of variations, but the end result is the same. The serum is carried through the body but absorption is so minimal that the effect is non-existent."

Becca spent the next few hours sharing the results of the hundreds of tests she had completed. She was hoping they would find the anomaly that was preventing the absorption.

"Becca, what is this, what is this spike in number 99?" Dr. Levin lifted the piece of paper and held it to the light. "This interests me; I have not seen this spike in any of the other results. What change did you make that would cause such a spike?"

Becca pulled the file on test 99 and reviewed her notes. "It's similar to the one before, but my notes indicate that 99 was a failure. The spike was from overheating the enzyme mixture past 104 degrees; in fact, my records show the temperature reading was 111 degrees. I ran the test and figured it was useless because I had let the enzyme get too hot."

"Here, young Becca, look here," Dr. Levin pointed at the graph.

"It's been under my nose the entire time, but I only saw a mistake, I never studied the results, I never thought..." Becca paused, looking at Dr. Levin with a smile, "I never thought to look further."

"We need to recreate that day, Becca. This is one time you want to make the same mistake twice." Dr. Levin stood up and put his hand on her shoulder. "Your Father would be very proud Becca, very proud."

Becca and the Doctor worked together to recreate the results from test 99. The sun was setting when Jack walked in and startled Becca. She dropped her pen and watched as it slipped through the crack in the floor. "Oh no, that was my favorite pen."

Jack laughed. "I told you to watch the cracks in the floor." He glanced around the room and in a more serious tone added, "Becca, it's time, we need to go."

Jack knew the window was closing and the crew with Agent Branson had reported no sign of Nilov. If Nilov was as good as Jack knew him to be, he may have figured out that Agent Branson was a decoy and would not be far from finding them.

Moscow was a big city, but Nilov's network reached far. He had inserted himself deeply into the underground network and for a price; he could buy just about anything or anyone.

"Jack, we are so close, we need more time," Becca said as she looked at Jack with determination in her eyes.

"Thirty minutes, that's all, Becca, and that's pushing it," he reluctantly responded, knowing the longer they stayed there, the more danger they were in.

"Thirty minutes? We need more and..." was all she was able to say before Jack cut her off.

"That's it, not one minute more."

Dr. Levin stood up and in his low Russian voice offered her reassurance. "We will be okay, we can finish, we are close."

Both Dr. Levin and Becca watched as the temperature reading climbed to 109, 110, and then 111. They quickly completed the mixture, making sure the temperature didn't waiver from 111 degrees. Once the mixture bonded, they moved the vial to the cooling cabinet to bring it down to 98.6 degrees, the same as the human body. Becca took the vial from the cooling cabinet and extracted the serum into a syringe. She carefully placed a small amount on the test slide and placed it in the analyzer.

"Now we wait," Dr. Levin said as he and Becca intently stared at the timer on the analyzer; neither said a word as they listened to it cycle through the process.

Becca slowly approached the results screen as the timer wound down to zero. She was afraid to look, afraid of the disappointment she would feel if number 99 was a failure. Taking a deep breath, Becca lifted her head to read the results.

By the look on her face, Dr. Levin knew, but needed confirmation. "It's good, yes, Becca?"

"It's more than good; it's Gen-E, she's here, right here." Becca looked at the clock to mark the time. Tears welled up in her eyes as she remembered her father and how much this moment would have meant to him.

"We did it, Doctor, after all these years here she is, we found her!" Becca was so immersed in results she did not even see Dr. Levin walk to the window and unlock it.

"I'm sorry, young Becca," he said as he stood to the side of the window.

Becca looked up from the screen to see Dr. Levin standing next to the open window; he was as white as a ghost and clasping his hands tightly together. "Doctor, what's wrong? Why are you sorry?" She stared at him for just a moment, her eyes shifting to the figure entering through the window.

"Jack, Jack!" Becca screamed as she ran for the lab table. She knew what they were there for and she was going to make sure they didn't get it. Becca reached for the pre-serum mixture and knowing from experience that it was extremely flammable, she smashed it on the lab table and tipped over the burner setting the entire table on fire.

"Becca, no, you don't understand! What have you done?" Dr. Levin yelled as a second, very large man came through the window.

Not understanding why Dr. Levin would compromise Gen-E, Becca stood there watching the fire burn her research and engulf her computer. Knowing she didn't have much time, she slid her hand in her pocket and prayed she hit the right button. If she did, the synch would only take seconds and Gen-E would be safely stored on her phone.

Becca squinted through the haze of smoke building in the lab and recognized one of the men from the pictures Jack had shown her on the plane; it was Maxim Binovich, the man that had taken the picture of her and her father in New York.

Binovich pointed his gun at Dr. Levin, "What now, Doc?"

Dr. Levin watched as the fire engulfed Gen-E, the one thing that would buy his freedom and allow him to find his daughter. "No, no, please no!" He held his head in his hands in disbelief.

Becca ran to the analyzer, grabbed the slide with the serum and threw it into the flames. Seeing the anger in Binovich's eyes, she slowly backed away from the fire bumping up against the lab table behind her. There, just inches from her hand, was the syringe. Her instinct to save the serum was strong, but her need to keep Gen-E out of the hands of the Russians was stronger. She knew if she didn't act fast, Binovich would get his hands on the serum. Her thoughts were almost screaming in her head to throw it in the fire.

Binovich pointed the gun at Dr. Levin, "Doc, there had better be more than what's burning."

"You're working with them?" Becca yelled at Dr. Levin. She didn't know why, but she could clearly see the sadness and defeat in his eyes.

"Young Becca, you don't understand, you don't know what I have been through to get here. Yes, I made a deal with the devil, but only to finally meet the daughter I never knew I had."

Binovich was frustrated at the exchange of sentiment and pushed the gun tight against Dr. Levin's head.

"Wait, don't shoot! There, over there, the serum, there's some left in the syringe!" Dr. Levin yelled as he pointed at the lab table behind Becca.

Becca cupped the syringe in her hand and slid it behind her leg. She never even felt the needle go in, nor did she care that she was injecting herself with something that had never been fully tested. It was her only way to preserve her father's work and to keep it from Binovich. She pulled out the syringe and let go, watching it fall through the crack in the floor. It was somewhere far below and would be buried forever when the building was demolished.

Binovich ran over to the table and pushed Becca out of the way, he searched the table dumping out the boxes of supplies and pushing the equipment on the floor. "There is no syringe!" He turned to Becca, pointing the gun at her. "Where is it?"

Becca knew she had to make him believe her. "I don't know what you are talking about, there isn't any syringe."

Dr. Levin ran toward the fire, "There was a syringe, she must have thrown it in the fire. Quickly find it before it's ruined!"

Becca heard the shot and saw Dr. Levin fall to the floor. She screamed. "Why? He's just a doctor!" She ran to him and checked for a pulse but knew he was dead. She looked directly at Binovich. "He was a scientist, he did you no harm, now it's lost, it's all lost."

"I would not speak so quickly, Doctor. I have you and you can fix this. You will fix this." He waived the gun at her. "Get up, we are leaving and you are coming with us."

Becca began to stand up when she heard another shot and felt the immense weight of the other large Russian as they fell to the floor, his dead body pinning her to the ground.

Binovich ran to the side of the room hiding behind a concrete pillar. He scanned the room looking for where the shot had come from.

Jack watched from the opening in the ceiling above and waited for a clear shot at Binovich. The smoke from the fire was getting thicker and the fire was growing. Jack had to do something fast or Becca would die. He shot again hitting the concrete pillar Binovich was hiding behind and strained to see through the smoke as Binovich made his way toward Becca.

The heat from the fire shattered the container at the end of the lab table sending flames to the ceiling. Jack rolled away as the flames shot past his head. He knew it was a matter of seconds before it would be too late. He moved to his right, straining to see through a small gap in the floor, but the smoke was too thick. Time stopped for just that moment when he heard the shot, then silence. He was too late, it was over and Nilov's far reaching hand had once again taken someone from Jack.

He laid there as the night before flashed through his mind; remembering her touch, her kiss, and her sweet smile. He pounded his head with his fist, she didn't deserve to die.

"Jack, Jack, help!" Becca screamed.

"Becca?" He yelled back.

"Jack! Help!"

Jack ran to the other end of the room above the lab and jumped to one of the open ceiling beams, hanging just long enough to see a clearing in the smoke as he dropped to the lab floor.

Becca was lying on the floor pinned under the Russian and holding a gun in her hand. "I shot at him Jack, but I don't know if I hit him. He went out the window."

Jack pulled the Russian off Becca and helped her to her feet. "You shot at Binovich?"

"Yeah, this guy's gun was sitting on the floor at my side and when I saw Binovich, I just grabbed it and shot."

"Well you did enough to scare him off. Now let's get you out of here."

Jack held Becca close as they made their way down the stairs and into the alley. They could hear the fire engine sirens fast approaching. Jack guided Becca through the crowded sidewalks back to the hotel parking garage. As they left the structure and pulled into traffic, she could see the smoke billowing out the building windows just a few blocks away. Even though he betrayed her, Becca's heart was heavy knowing Dr. Levin lost his life and would never get the chance to meet his daughter.

Becca stared out the window of the plane as it flew over Moscow en route to the States. The city looked different now; it was no longer somewhere she wanted to return, ever.

"Jack, do you ever get over it?"

"Over what?"

"Killing someone; I know I didn't kill Binovich, but I could have."

"You did what you had to, Becca, it was you or him, and I am thankful you did what you did."

"What scares me is that it wasn't even a conscious choice, I just did it."

"Instinct to survive, we all have it and we all use it when we need to, and you needed to." Jack was trying to assure Becca that she did what anyone would have done in the same situation.

"Yeah, I guess you're right, but it still doesn't make me feel any better." She laid her head on the pillow and drifted off to sleep.

Jack was too wound up to sleep; he went over the plan a million times, blaming himself for allowing Binovich to get so close to Becca. Even though for just a moment, he thought Becca was dead, he never wanted to feel that again, and knew he had to do everything in his power to keep Becca safe. He gently covered her with a blanket and let her sleep for most of the flight. Jack couldn't deny the strong attraction he had and for the first time in his life, he could picture himself settling down.

Becca was just barely awake and could hear Jack talking to someone. She opened her eyes to see Jack on the phone at the front of the plane.

"Agent Branson and her team are due to arrive back at the base tomorrow. I included her debrief with mine." Jack paused for a moment, "I understand, Sir, I will let the Doc know." Jack hung up the phone and ran his fingers through his hair.

"Let me know what, Jack?"

He walked over and sat down next to Becca. "That was Brach, they reviewed the debrief and ..." Jack hesitated to continue.

"What? Just spit it out."

"The Agency is shutting down the Gen-E Project. The Russian Government is trying to figure out how Nilov got to Dr. Levin and they're cleaning up the mess Nilov left when he took out the team escorting the Doctor to Moscow. The Agency needs to let things cool down, and when it's safe, they'll bring you in to discuss the future of the The Gen-E Project. Right now, they are hearing chatter that Nilov's attention is focused on you. He's not the kind of guy that accepts defeat."

Becca felt a sense of relief. After what she had been though, after all she and her father had given up for the project, she was ready to experience life outside of Gen-E. "It's okay, Jack, just means more time for treasure hikes." She managed a slight smile and hoped the end of the project didn't mean the end of them.

Jack was thinking the same thing. "You know the Agency mandates leave after a mission with human casualty. How about I take you up on teaching me to find treasure, and you keep your end of the bargain and learn how to dive?"

Becca didn't hesitate in her response. "It's a deal."

CHAPTER 6

THE PORCH OF THE SMALL oceanfront cottage overlooked a short path to the ocean and had just enough space for a lounge chair and table on each end. A hammock hung between two large palm trees at the end of the path that opened up to a beautiful sandy beach. To the east was the marina and in the opposite direction were the tourist-filled resorts of the small island. It didn't matter that the cottage lacked all the conveniences Jack and Becca had grown accustomed to; no dishwasher, no air conditioning, no cable TV. It was the perfect place for them to get away, to put Moscow behind them.

Becca was sitting comfortably on the front porch as Jack made his way up the path from the beach. She quickly closed her laptop and focused her attention on how incredibly good Jack looked at that moment, wearing just his shorts and carrying a metal detector. With the ocean in the background, his golden tan and infectious smile reminded her how lucky she was to be with him.

"Look what I found," he said holding out his hand.

"Let me guess, another beer can?" Becca laughed as she stood up and walked down the steps to take a look.

"Close your eyes," he said as he placed what he had found in her hand.

Becca opened her eyes and looked down at the ring; it was beautiful, and very old. The gold shimmered in the sunlight and the small red stones peeked through the silt build up from years in the ocean.

Jack was proud of his find and knew it would impress even the best treasure hunter.

"So now who's the king of treasure?"

Becca had a story for everything they would find, she could imagine where it came from, who owned it and why it was lost. "It's beautiful, Jack, and really old, I bet it came from a woman of royalty, she must have been very beautiful to have a ring like this from her husband."

Jack continued the story line. "She was sailing to the Americas to join her husband when her ship was caught in a fierce storm and she was thrown overboard, never to be seen again. He awaited her arrival and was devastated by the news of his wife's death. Filled with grief, he ran into the sea to find her, but never returned."

Becca listened to Jack tell the story, amazed by his imagination. It was a side of Jack she had not seen before.

"This sea air suits you well, Jack," she said leaning in to kiss him.

"I think it does, too." He took the ring from her hand. "Let me clean this up to get a better look at it."

Becca watched as Jack walked back into the house tossing and catching the ring a few times in triumph. She opened her laptop studying the results of her blood tests. There were no variations, no anomalies, and no indication that the serum had affected her at all. She breathed a sigh of relief; it was the eighth test and she was satisfied now that she was in the clear, but felt a bit of disappointment the serum had not produced the results she had expected. She filed the results away in an obscure folder on her laptop, leaned back in the chair to enjoy the early evening breeze and drifted off to sleep.

Jack had been patient teaching Becca over the past two months and she was feeling much more comfortable with diving. The sun was directly above when Becca and Jack set out for the reef just off the coast. They spent an hour exploring when Jack signaled Becca it was time to go. As they rose to the surface, Becca admired the way the light changed with every swell on the surface. The world was different under the water; it was peaceful and welcoming and gave her the feeling of tranquility. She wondered how she could have ever been afraid.

As they reached the surface, Becca knew why Jack wanted to go. The storm building in the open water to the west was already providing two foot swells, and by the looks of the approaching dark clouds it was only going to get worse. They made it back to the marina before the storm hit, but couldn't avoid the downpour on the way to the car. Sitting in the car they were both dripping wet. Jack looked at Becca in admiration. "You're beautiful."

"Oh yeah, about as beautiful as a drowned rat I expect." She replied, trying to dry her hair with one of the half-soaked beach towels.

He grabbed the towel, pulling it away from her face, and kissed her. "Let's go back out tomorrow if the weather is better. I want to take another look at that reef."

"Perfect." Becca said, but was referring to more than another dive; she meant everything about her life, right now, in this moment, was absolutely perfect.

※

The afternoon storms had filled the western horizon with large white puffy clouds hanging just above the water line creating the most beautiful sunset Becca had ever seen.

"Can we just capture this moment in time and save it for a rainy day?" she said as she stared at the ocean watching the orange and pink colors of the sunset dance along the waves.

Jack held her a little closer, rocking the hammock back and forth. He turned and kissed Becca, moving her hair away from her eyes. He loved her more than life itself, there isn't anything he wouldn't do for her. They had spent the two months since Moscow completely cut off from the rest of the world, bringing them closer together than either of them could have imagined.

Becca's love for Jack was intense. She was no longer able to see life without him, every thought of her future included Jack, a future that was about to change.

"I love you, Jack," she said in an emotional and soft voice as she rested her head on Jack's chest.

"I love you, too, Becca."

"But do you love all of me?"

"Of course, every inch."

Becca reached over and grabbed Jack's hand, setting it gently on her belly. "Good, because there's going to be more of me to love Jack, in fact, there is going to be a lot more."

Jack's hand spread out over her belly, his heart pounding.

"We're having a baby, Jack."

He gently rubbed her belly. "A little Jack running around would be the all the treasure I ever need."

"A little Jackie would be even better," she said as she put her hand on top of his.

"Becca, you have brought out the best in me, you have changed my life, and only one thing could make me happier than I am right now. Marry me, marry me, Becca." Jack slipped a ring on her finger.

She looked down to see the ring Jack had found on the beach. It was perfect. She ran her finger across the shimmering red jewels. "Yes Jack, I will marry you."

They stayed there, swinging in the hammock until the last sliver of sun was visible on the horizon. No words could possibly explain how perfect a moment it was.

Becca had gone for a run on the beach the next morning. Walking back up the porch steps she could hear men's voices coming from the cottage. They had not had any visitors to their beach hideaway and their neighbors were too far away to drop in for a visit. She stepped to the side of the porch trying to listen to the conversation. She was relieved to hear Jack laugh and curious to know who was there, who could have known where they were.

"Morning," she said to Jack and the two men sitting at the kitchen table as she walked in the kitchen.

The talking stopped, and both the men looked at Becca, then at Jack.

Jack turned to Becca with a smile. "Becca, this is Sharpe and ZMan, two of the most obnoxious pain in the ass agents you will ever meet."

They all laughed and both Sharpe and ZMan stood up to shake Becca's hand.

"Nice to meet you, Becca," said ZMan. He was a good looking man, with longer dark hair, a mustache and overly large biceps. His t-shirt gave away his love for boating with a sailboat and tag line that said 'I'd rather be sailing'.

"Doctor, a pleasure," Sharpe's hand shake was strong, his hand wrapping all the way around Becca's.

"Hungry, guys?" Becca asked as she opened the fridge.

"Don't know about you guys, but I'm starving," Sharp quickly replied.

Becca could see why, he was well over six feet and must spend hours in the gym to look like he does. She wondered if he still worked for the Agency since his appearance wasn't like the other agents Becca knew. Tattoos covered both his arms, his head was shaven and if she had to guess, she would have pegged him as a biker, not a Federal Agent. Sitting down at the table, Becca listened to the three guys talk about the past, being careful not to share too much detail.

"Hey Doc, we brought you a present," ZMan said as he put a gift bag on the table.

Jack laughed. "Oh, this is going to be good."

Becca reached in and pulled out a gold fire extinguisher with instructions for use engraved in large print on the front.

"You guys are too much," Becca said as she turned a light shade of pink.

"Oh don't be embarrassed, Doc, you provided us with the best opportunity to harass Lyndo," Sharpe said hitting, Jack on the back.

Jack smiled. "You know, guys; she could be arrested for possession of a deadly weapon."

"I'll be happy to take her in," ZMan quickly responded.

"Not a chance," Jack replied.

Becca stood up to clear the dishes, but Jack put his hand on her arm to stop her. "I think you need to sit down. There is something you should know."

Becca slowly sat back down, looking at Jack, then Sharpe, then ZMan. They went from laughing about the fire extinguisher to quiet and serious. ZMan had a hard time making eye contact. "What's going on guys?" Becca asked.

Sharpe began first. "It's Nilov, he's back on the radar, and this time he is serious about finding you. He was able to recover your laptop and some of the information on it."

ZMan stepped in. "Becca, he needs someone to fill in the gaps and knows you are the only one who can do that."

For the first time since Moscow, Becca was scared. "We're safe here right, Jack?"

Jack reached over and grabbed her hand. "We're not, we need to go, and we need to go today."

"What? Today? Why today?"

Sharpe's tone was low and stern. "Doc, Binovich is here, he is in the States and we believe he is here for one reason, to find you."

The memory of that night flashed through her mind. "Jack, he found me twice, he can find me again. If you know he is here, why can't you find him?"

"We are working on it, but we need to use caution, he is not someone to mess around with. We need to be sure we can detain him, which means he needs to make a mistake here, in the US," ZMan said. "We'll get him, Becca, we will, I promise."

Jack looked at Becca. "We need to pack; we're leaving with Sharpe and ZMan. I'm sorry, Becca, but we have no choice. We'll go to the base where it's safe; that will give us time to plan our next move. We're not safe here, Becca, not with Binovich in the States."

CHAPTER 7

THE WALK FROM temporary housing to the Doctor's office at the base hospital was just over a half mile and allowed Becca time to think. It wasn't the beach, but she knew it was where they needed to be for now.

The streets all looked the same; each house was the same color, the same size, the same layout. The only thing different was the address on the mailbox, which she had memorized and could recite with her eyes closed. It had been months since they moved to the base and her due date was fast approaching. It wasn't where she had pictured having a baby, but she understood why they were there.

Jack, Sharpe and ZMan worked relentlessly on finding Binovich, but lost him in Miami. The search was taking longer than they had hoped, and for

Becca's safety, it was important they stay at the base until Binovich was either dead, in custody, or back in Russia.

Dr. Frank walked in the exam room. "Morning Becca, how are you feeling today?"

Becca liked her Doctor, he was the one person she could talk to on a regular basis and the conversations were about regular everyday life.

"I'm feeling great, Dr. Frank, just anxious to see if we are having a boy or a girl."

"Is Jack joining us today?"

"I am," Jack replied as he came through the door.

Dr. Frank began the ultrasound and didn't say much for the first few minutes, making both Jack and Becca a bit nervous. They didn't care if it was a boy or a girl, as long as the baby was healthy.

"Everything looks great. However, development seems to be a bit advanced which may push your due date up a bit. She will be here before you know it," he said smiling at Becca.

"A girl, Jack, it's a girl!"

Tears filled Becca's eyes as Jack leaned over and kissed her forehead. "She will never date, I hope you know. Never!"

Jack's phone rang. "It's Sharpe, I have to take this Becca, and I'll be right outside."

Becca trusted Dr. Frank; they had built a friendship since she and Jack had arrived at the base. The ultrasound confirming that the baby was okay offered relief to Becca, but the lingering thought of the injection the day after conception was always in the back of Becca's mind. She had never told Jack for fear of his reaction, and she knew from the test results there had been no effect on her. With Dr. Frank's observation of advanced development, she needed to know what effect, if any, it may have on their daughter.

"Dr. Frank, are you able to run genetic testing at this stage, just to make sure everything is okay?" Becca asked.

"We usually don't unless we have a reason to test, like family history or previous pregnancy issues."

Becca knew she could not tell Dr. Frank why she wanted the test, but she had to know if the injection had any effect on her daughter. Finding out now would give her time to tell Jack, and more importantly, give her time to accept the fact that she may have done something to jeopardize her daughter's life. "I would like an amniocentesis procedure, just to take a look at the enzymes, proteins and analyze the cells, is that possible?"

Dr. Frank looked at Becca, surprised to hear Becca ask such a medically pointed question. "Sounds like someone did a little too much internet research; you can't believe everything you read, Becca."

She had to convince Dr. Frank to do the procedure without sharing too much information. "I know, Dr. Frank, but there is history of Cystic Fibrosis on my side of the family and I just want to be sure."

"You know that both parents must pass on the defective gene for a child to get the disease? I don't see anything in the file to indicate either of you have a history."

Becca wasn't going to take no for an answer. "I didn't think of it when I filled out the paperwork, and Jack doesn't have much health history from his side of the family. His parents passed away when he was very young."

"Well then, I will order the test. Stop by the front desk on your way out to set up the appointment. When I get the results, I will give you a call." Dr. Frank wrote the order and handed it to Becca.

It seemed like an eternity waiting for the results of the procedure. Becca made sure she was first to answer the phone and first to check the answering machine so Jack wouldn't find out. She didn't want to explain why, not until she knew the results. It wasn't easy for Becca to keep this from Jack; she had always been honest with him, but this time she needed to make sure she knew the answers before he started asking questions.

The sound of the lawnmower overpowered the TV, so Becca walked over to close the front door when the phone rang. She looked at the caller ID; it was Dr. Frank. She took a deep breath and on the third ring she answered.

"Hi Becca, it's Dr. Frank, I have the results of the amniocentesis procedure. Good news, there is no sign of Cystic Fibrosis."

"That's great, Dr. Frank." Becca already knew it would come back negative. She was more interested in any other genetic abnormalities and had to get the doctor to share more of the results. "What else did the test results show?"

"Everything came back pretty normal; however, there was one test that showed an interesting departure from the norm. I have seen these tests come back with similar results before and never had any adverse outcome, meaning that the test results didn't prove to be accurate once the child was born. Not to worry, Becca, really."

She was more curious now. She needed to know the exact result he was talking about, she needed to know if what she had done affected the baby in any way. "Dr. Frank, what test are you referring to?"

"It's not the test specifically, but a result within the genetic test showing a variation of the calcitonin gene."

"Was it a positive or negative variation, Dr. Frank?" she asked, without realizing her line of questioning would certainly give Dr. Frank cause for concern.

"Becca, why the interest in this test? It's most likely just an error. Genetic testing is not a perfect science."

"Dr. Frank, I'm just super interested in the health of my daughter and want to know the specifics. Can you tell me if it was a positive or negative variation?"

"It was a positive, and a rather large positive variation at that. But Becca, don't let it alarm you; this type of variation is not one for concern. I would certainly tell you if it was."

"How big of a positive variation?" she blurted out the question completely focused on the results and oblivious to the fact that she was digging a bit too deep with Dr. Frank.

"87% above main." He responded with a confused tone not understanding why Becca was going down this path of questioning.

"Thank you, Dr. Frank, see you next week." Becca hung up the phone and stood there in shock. She fully understood the results even if Dr. Frank did not. She wasn't afraid; he was correct in his assumption that the variation wasn't a concern from a medical standpoint, but from her perspective, it meant she was carrying more than a baby; she was carrying Gen-E. She paced nervously back and forth trying to figure out what she was going to say to Jack, and how she was going to tell him their daughter was going to be different, very different.

Dr. Frank was puzzled by Becca's interest in the results and curious with her persistence in knowing the positive or negative variation. He was even more alarmed when she asked for the variation percentage. He knew there were very few people in the world that would care about the variation, much less understand what it meant. He didn't know enough about this test or how the results would impact an unborn child and would have shrugged off the results as an error. But this time, he wanted to know more, he wanted to understand Becca's line of questioning.

He picked up the phone and called Dr. Li Peng, an associate working with Cayton Pharmaceuticals Genetic Research Division in Philadelphia.

"Dr. Peng, Dr. Edwin Frank from the US Army Fort Bragg. You and I had the chance to work together about ten years ago on the Frontier Project."

"Hello, Ed. How are you these days?"

"Good, thanks. Sorry to call you out of the blue, but my curiosity has gotten the best of me on a genetic test result from one of my patients, and I am pretty sure you can provide some of the insight."

Dr. Frank explained how Becca had pushed for the test with no documented family history and explained the variation in the calcitonin gene, along with Becca's direct and very pointed questions.

"I was going to shrug it off as a testing error, but my patient's persistent questioning made me want to dig a bit deeper."

Dr. Peng was silent for a moment, responding with a quiet, serious tone. "You say she asked for the percentage of variation?"

"Yes, she did."

"Ed, there are only a handful of people in this world that would ask that question. Is your patient a research scientist?"

"No Li, she's the wife of one of the enlisted here on the base. Is the result one I should be concerned about?"

"No Ed, not the result, it's not going to cause harm to the child, but I would be concerned about your patient's level of knowledge on the results. See what more you can find out about your patient. Dig a bit to see if she was involved in any type of genetic research or exposed to anything that would cause this type of fluctuation."

"I'll do that, Li, and when I find out more, I'll give you a ring."

Dr. Frank hung up the phone and logged into the patient records system to look at Becca's history in an attempt to identify anything that would give him answers. He clicked on the link to review the test results again. He called his assistant, "Kate, is there a problem with the patient records system?"

"Not that I am aware of. I'm in the system now and it seems to be working fine, why?" Kate asked.

"I'm looking at a patient's test results and they are different than they were earlier today. Have you had this happen before?"

"No. Never. I'm not even sure how that could happen," she said.

"Okay, if you hear about any issues, let me know." He hung up the phone and stared at the screen. Becca's results were completely normal and the calcitonin variation was gone. He sat back in his chair wondering if the computer made a mistake or if he did and hoped he hadn't given Becca false information. He would wait until tomorrow to check the results again before calling Becca.

Dr. Frank arrived home that evening and heard voices from the patio. He walked through the house to the back door to see his wife sitting on the patio talking to Jack.

"Hi honey. Agent Lyndon stopped in to chat with you and I told him he could wait."

Dr. Frank was surprised and uncomfortable that Jack had come to his home. "Hello, Jack."

"Sorry to stop unannounced. I will just take a few minutes of your time," Jack said as he looked intently at Dr. Frank.

Maggie could tell it was not a conversation she was meant to be a part of. "I'll let you guys talk, it was nice to meet you, Jack."

"You too, Maggie, thanks for the tea." Jack motioned for Dr. Frank to sit down. "Ed, I need you to listen very carefully. The results you gave to my wife today can never be discussed with anyone, ever. Your call to Dr. Peng today put both of you in danger."

Dr. Frank was stunned by the fact that Jack knew about the call to Dr. Peng. "But the results were wrong, they are normal. I checked again this afternoon before I came home."

"They are normal because I made them normal, and if ever questioned, you will continue to say they were normal," Jack said with authority.

Dr. Frank was obviously nervous. "I don't understand."

"You don't need to understand, what you need to know is that you and your wife are being relocated to another base, and you are leaving tonight. The agents will be here in two hours to take you to the airstrip. When you get on the plane they will tell you where you are going. I suggest you don't give anyone the details of your relocation, not even your wife. She's going to have to trust you and understand you don't have a choice."

"What's going to happen to Dr. Peng?" he asked.

"Agents are en route. I just hope they get there first," Jack said as he stood up.

"Oh my God, I hope nothing happens to him. He is a great man and a brilliant scientist." Dr. Frank hung his head in disbelief then looked back up at Jack. "I would ask who you really are, who your wife really is, but I am guessing it's above my rank."

"That's right, Ed, and its better you know no more than you already do." Jack started walking toward the driveway, stopping briefly to give Dr. Frank his final instructions. "You need to worry about you and your wife, you need to follow direction and don't deviate from the plan. Her life is in your hands, protect her by keeping quiet and forgetting you ever had Becca as a patient."

Becca was pacing back and forth in the living room waiting for Jack to come home. She knew she had to tell him, she just wasn't sure what to say, or how he would react. She was worried about how he would feel finding out she had not told him about the serum injection before. She heard his car pull in the driveway and her heart was pounding as she watched him walk to the door. "Hi, Jack," she said nervously as he turned the corner into the living room.

"Jack we need to talk. I, I, I need to tell you something," she said as she down on the couch.

Jack walked over and handed Becca a folder. "Would it have anything to do with this?"

Becca opened the folder and read the first page; it was the test results showing the calcitonin levels. "How did you find out?"

"Becca, your life and the life of our daughter is at stake. Don't you think that I would take every precaution to ensure your safety?"

"I'm sorry, I'm sorry for not telling you sooner." Jack was angry and it was the first time she had seen this side of him.

"Just so you know the impact of not telling me; Dr. Frank and his wife are being relocated as we speak, and the doctor that he called today is nowhere to be found. Not to mention that Sharpe had to pay a visit to the testing lab to erase any record of your tests and ZMan hacked the medical records to change the results so they appeared normal. Becca, I cannot protect you and our daughter if you're not completely honest with me."

"I didn't realize, Jack, and I was afraid to tell you. I didn't know how," she said as the tears streamed down her face.

"Tell me what, what is it that you have been hiding? Why would Dr. Frank call Dr. Peng and what do these test results mean?" Jack was firing off question after question.

"Dr. Peng, he called Dr. Peng?" Becca was aware of Dr. Peng. He had worked with her father early in his career and Becca knew Dr. Peng's reputation for controversial genetic testing. "Dr. Peng is missing?"

"Yes, Becca, he is. The Agency is looking for him, but isn't having much luck."

"How? How did they know?"

"Nilov and his team have their eyes on anyone that could help them get the Gen-E project finished. They are watching the top genetic research labs in the world, hoping for a break, and they got that today."

Becca sat there silent, wondering how things had gotten so out of control. She wanted to help the world, and instead she was putting people's lives in danger, including her daughter's.

Jack sat down next to Becca. He knew he had been harsh on her, but he was doing what he does best, protecting those around him. "Becca, I need to know the truth. What do those test results really mean?"

"The night in the lab, Dr. Levin was fighting for his life and I could see the fear in his eyes as he watched the research go up in flames. He was a pawn for Nilov and he knew if he didn't give them Gen-E, he would be of no use to them. I had a choice, throw the only remaining evidence of Gen-E in the fire, or, or ... take it with me. I chose to take it with me."

"What do you mean you took it with you?"

"There was a syringe I used in the test; it was sitting next to me on the lab table, it all happened so fast." Becca buried her face in her hands frozen in fear to tell him the truth.

"Becca, what happened so fast, what the hell happened?"

She looked up at Jack and blurted out the truth. "I injected it in my leg and dropped the syringe through the crack in the floor."

By the look of complete shock on Jack's face she knew she had to explain. "I would have never done it had I known I was pregnant, I didn't know. I wasn't worried about me. I tested my blood many times while we were in the Keys and it showed no signs of change, no effect at all."

"Until now, and not to you, but to our daughter. Becca, is that what the test results show, is our daughter carrying Gen-E?"

"I believe she is, but there is nothing to worry about, the results are not harmful to the baby."

"Becca, I believe you when you say our daughter will be fine. It's Nilov I am worried about. He knows she is carrying Gen-E, which makes her more of a target than you."

Becca rubbed her belly telling her unborn daughter how sorry she was for putting her in harm's way before she was even born and promising to protect her and make sure she had the most normal life they could possibly give her.

"We have a very small window of opportunity," Jack said as he opened the wall safe and sifted through the various passports and removed the few bundles of cash he had stashed for an emergency.

"For what, Jack? Opportunity for what?"

"We need to move, we need to start over. It's not just Nilov that will be looking for us; the Agency is going to want us too."

"Jack, you know if either of them finds us, her life will be over before it has even started." Becca was devastated; she had no intention of allowing anyone, even the Agency, to use her daughter as a research project.

Jack did what Jack does best; in less than three hours they were gone without a trace. The house and bank accounts were empty, the medical records erased, the cell phones discarded, and every electronic device wiped clean.

CHAPTER 8

SHARPE STOOD AT THE SMALL rest area watching as the sun hit the horizon and the sky darkened. The outline of the trees against the fading blue background was all he could make out when the headlights approached slowly into the rest area.

Jack was thankful Sharpe agreed to meet him, but knew he was putting Sharpe in danger. "Did you bring everything?" Jack asked as he walked to the trunk of Sharpe's car.

"Yeah, I got it all." Sharpe lifted the black bags out of his trunk and set them on the tailgate of Jack's truck.

Jack opened the first bag containing new passports, IDs and birth certificates for Jack and Becca; then went through the second bag containing weapons, gear, a laptop, surveillance equipment, and tracking devices. The third bag was smaller and held just three blue canisters clearly marked with the toxic symbol.

"That's some nasty shit, Jack, don't mess around with that, it'll eat clear down to the bone."

Jack gently put the canisters back in the bag and pulled out the rolled up documents. "Are these recent?"

"Is yesterday recent enough for you?"

"Perfect." Jack quickly looked through the blueprints, rolled them back up and set them on the front seat. As he turned toward the back of the truck he could see Sharpe digging in his trunk.

"Jack, this was the biggest pain in the ass to get and I'm wondering why the hell you needed this old go kart gas tank." Sharpe said as he set the old rusty tank on the tailgate. "You know the Agency is all over your property?"

"Yeah, I know, but this was a matter of survival." Jack grabbed a screwdriver out of his toolbox and pried open the fake cap he had attached to the tank. Reaching inside he pulled out one of the large roles of hundred-dollar bills, neatly packaged in a small baggie.

"Make sense now?" Jack tossed the baggie at Sharpe. "You keep that, there is plenty more for me."

"You always did prepare for the worst, props to you man. You need some help on this one, Lyndo?"

"Thanks man, but I think I'll fly solo. You've done enough and I don't want to see you risk your career for this."

"You could just walk away, Jack. You know they would never find you."

"I don't have a choice; I have to throw a few roadblocks their way to slow them down. I'd rather have the attention focused in Richmond and on the Agency, than on us."

Sharpe had never seen Jack look so intense, but he understood why. This time was different, this time the mission was personal. It wasn't some random asset, this time it was his family he was protecting.

"If anything ever happens to me, you take this and you use it as a bargaining chip, this is Becca's and my daughter's ticket to freedom. You get them out of here, you protect them. Promise me you will watch over them," Jack said as he slipped a microchip in Sharpe's shirt pocket.

"You got it, Lyndo. Is this the formula?"

"It's just a copy of Becca's research; I got it in Russia before we left to meet with Dr. Levin so it doesn't have the final formula, but it has enough of Gen-E to be valuable. Becca doesn't know I copied her laptop so it's safer if you keep it, and right now, the Agency has the same research. They will never leave us alone if all they need is Becca to give them what she found in Russia. But without any trace of

Gen-E, the Agency is going to have to start over and they will have a hard time explaining the need for that kind of funding. If I am lucky, the committee will scrap the entire project and Gen-E will be a distant memory. That microchip will be priceless and the only thing that will be left when I'm finished."

"How's Becca holding up?"

"She's scared; she's worried about the baby."

Sharpe pulled out a piece of paper and handed it to Jack. "Here take this; you are going to need it."

Jack read the name on the piece of paper; "Laura Neumann, Pierce, Idaho."

"She's some kind of midwife; she can deliver the baby without being in a hospital, and let's just say, she owes me big time. You can trust her, Jack. Just stay away from the hospitals, the Agency is watching."

"I owe you, man." Jack shut the tailgate, shook Sharpe's hand and hopped in the truck.

"No you don't, we're even now." Sharpe said to himself as Jack drove away.

After Becca's father died, Jack was reassigned to Asset Recovery and the team was on what they thought would be a simple recovery mission just like all the rest. They had every expectation it would end with a successful asset extraction and with casualties. It wasn't often the Agency received bad intel, but for that Nicaraguan mission, the Agency got it wrong and it almost cost Sharpe his life.

Sharpe and ZMan were on point, Jack was their eyes and ears perched on a rooftop just 50 yards away. The asset was being held on the ground floor in the center of the compound, and by what their source had told them, there would be two armed men guarding the compound at the front gate. Jack located the guards and kept an eye on their movement as Sharpe and ZMan approached from opposite sides of the compound.

ZMan made his way over the wall and into the side door of the center building. Sharpe was moving around the back side of the first building when Jack saw the two armed guards approaching from the east; he looked back at the gate to see the two guards were still there. Jack radioed Sharpe to let him know there were two additional targets approaching when he heard the gun fire. Jack scanned the compound; the shots came from the outbuilding to the west of Sharpe. This wasn't what the Agency had been told, there were more guards in the compound than they anticipated and he knew Sharpe wasn't going to get out of there without help.

ZMan got to the asset and worked his way back through the corridors of the compound and into the alley. Within three minutes they made it to the extraction point. ZMan radioed Jack to let him know the asset was safe. Jack informed ZMan that Sharpe was under fire and confirmed the helicopter would be there in five minutes. He ordered ZMan to leave with the asset if he and Sharpe weren't there.

Jack radioed Sharpe, but no response. Sharpe took down the guard at the outbuilding as the other two guards turned the corner. Sharpe looked down at his hand and saw his gun lying on the ground. He never felt the bullet pass through his arm, but he could see the blood dripping on the gravel next to his foot. He reached down to pick it up, but his hand was useless. Sharpe felt the next hit and knew he was going down as the heat from the bullet seared through his side and into his back. Lying there on the ground he could hear the gun fire as he floated in and out of consciousness.

Sharpe's next memory was waking up in the base hospital hearing Jack and ZMan get their butts handed to them by the Captain as his voice echoed down the hospital hallway. "The decision was not yours to make. You broke mission protocol."

"Yes, Sir, with all due respect, Sir, the asset was clear. I saw the opportunity, I took it, Sir," Jack replied.

Jack's response angered the Captain even more. "You had orders and those orders did not include engaging in a gun battle leaving six dead guards. Hell, Jack, you started a fire storm down there and now the Agency is on damage control. You're damn lucky this ended the way it did."

The Captain's voice was so loud the doctor approached and asked him to move to a nearby waiting area. "I'll see both of you at Debrief. Dismissed."

Jack and ZMan watched as the ICU door closed behind the Captain.

Jack and ZMan walked into Sharpe's room.

"What the hell happened out there?" Sharpe asked.

"Seems like the Captain missed his happy pill today," ZMan said laughing, trying to make light of what had just happened.

"No man, what happened in Nicaragua? Where the hell did those guards come from?" Sharpe demanded to know.

"Don't know, man," Jack replied, "but they aren't going anywhere else, ever."

"Thanks, man, I owe you," Sharpe said as the pain meds kicked in and he drifted off to sleep.

Nicaragua was a long time ago, and now, Sharpe stood in the rest area parking lot watching Jack drive away. He knew there would come a time he would be able to repay Jack. He patted the shirt pocket that held the microchip Jack had just given him and hoped that it was not the last time he saw Lyndo.

CHAPTER 9

AGENT BRACH STARED out the window into the courtyard remembering his conversation with Becca. It was here that he last saw her.

Oblivious to the chaos going on around him, his thoughts focused on Becca and Jack. He knew they were in trouble and it was his job to find them. His orders were clear, get to Jack and Becca before Nilov did. What he didn't agree with was the hard-lined directive from the Agency to obtain the daughter of Jack and Becca Lyndon at any cost. Agent Brach was adamantly opposed to the fact that the Agency classified Jack and Becca as fugitives and their daughter an asset. Millions of dollars were invested in the project and the Agency felt justified in taking any means necessary to secure Gen-E.

The sergeant leading the search for evidence approached Agent Brach. "Sir, there is nothing here."

Agent Brach didn't respond.

"Sir?" The sergeant said again trying to get his attention.

"Find anything, Sergeant?" Agent Brach asked.

The sergeant handed Agent Brach a file. "No, Sir, nothing. We found information on other research the Doc was working on, but nothing on Gen-E."

"What about her house?"

"The team is still searching, Sir."

Irritated at the lack of results, Agent Brach responded with a harsh tone. "Well keep digging, there has to be something here. She worked for this Agency for years and her father for decades before that. Did you check all the backup systems, the lab hard drives, the off-site data storage?"

The sergeant could hear the frustration in Agent Brach's voice. "The lab and backup systems are clean, Sir. The data recovery team is at the off-site storage facility now; they should have results later today."

"I want those results, like yesterday, Sergeant. Make sure I am the first to know what they find, or with the pattern so far, what they don't find. You're dismissed, Sergeant."

Agent Brach sat down at Becca's desk and picked up the picture of her and her father. "Where is your daughter, Doc? I need some help here; I need to find them before Nilov does."

Agent Brach had forged a friendship with Becca's father outside of the Agency. The two had gone on annual deep sea fishing trips together; it was a passion for both of them. Becca's father wasn't a great fisherman, but he loved the open water and the freedom it offered from the concrete walls and demands of the lab. On the last trip together Becca's father caught a big marlin and fought for hours to reel it in. He finally got it close enough to the boat to get it on board, but the marlin still had some fight left in him and thrashed with enough energy that it pulled Becca's father in the ocean. Agent Brach never let him forget that day in Cabo and took every opportunity to joke about the marlin, the one that got away.

Assigned to Becca's father, Agent Brach accompanied him on many of the research trips before he brought Jack on board to take over. Agent Brach's promotion took him out of the field and put him behind a desk as Director of the Asset Protection division. He hand-selected Jack as his replacement and knew now that if Jack didn't want to be found, the Agency would never find him.

Agent Brach looked down at his phone, it was the sergeant calling. "Anything turn up at her house?"

"Clean again, Sir," the sergeant responded.

"I'll meet you at the data storage facility. Let's hope we don't come up empty there too." Agent Brach stood up and looked around Becca's office one last time.

He knew Jack was the only one who could have pulled off clearing all the Gen-E Project records and that it was Jack's way of stalling their investigation. The off-site data storage facility was the last opportunity to recover any kind of useful information and Agent Brach could only hope Jack was unable to bypass the security. He set the empty frame back on Becca's desk and slid the photo into his pocket speaking softly to himself as he walked out the door. "Let's hope Jack isn't my marlin."

The smoke was still hanging in the air as Agent Brach approached the corridor leading to the remote data storage building. He stepped over the fire-hoses and through puddles of water and could see the sergeant talking to one of the security guards at the end of the hall.

"What the hell happened here, Sergeant?" Agent Brach asked.

"Someone breached security, Sir, and did some pretty good damage."

"I can see that, Sergeant. How bad is it?"

The sergeant walked Agent Brach into the main data storage room that was lined end-to-end with tall dark cabinets and miles of cables and wires that ran up to the ceiling and over to the control panel. Agent Brach walked through the inch of water on the floor to a section of cabinets dripping in white foam.

"What's that white stuff, Sergeant?" Agent Brach asked as he covered his mouth with the end of his tie, "and what in the hell is that smell?"

The sergeant walked Agent Brach back out to the corridor explaining what he knew so far. "It's some kind of corrosion chemical, Sir, the team took a sample back to the lab to try and identify its origin. The water damage is minimal, the system is made to handle a certain amount of water, but the foam pretty much destroyed two of the Agency data racks. Whoever did this targeted the Agency and knew exactly what they were doing."

Agent Brach muttered under his breath as he walked back down the corridor. "Yeah it's a marlin."

"A what, Sir?" The sergeant questioned.

"You know, a marlin ... a fish, the one that got away."

The drive back to the Agency offered Agent Brach time to think, time to comprehend the danger Jack and Becca were in. Their daughter was the only remaining link to the Gen-E Project; he knew it, and soon enough the Russians would, too. He had to find them; it wasn't just his job that was driving him now, but his commitment to Becca's father to watch over her.

Agent Brach looked at his phone, it was the Major. "Hello, Sir."

"Brach, what the hell is going on?"

"Sir, we believe it was Agent Lyndon. The Gen-E project is gone, Sir, all of it." Agent Brach knew the news would not sit well with the Major.

"Not a smart move on his part. Was it, Agent Brach? Now he's put a target on his daughter's back. Hell, the Russians are going to be all over this and they won't stop until they find her."

"With all due respect, Sir, Agent Lyndon knows exactly what he is doing. He may have destroyed everything the Agency had, but he is smart enough to have insurance."

"Meaning what, Brach?"

"He's got Gen-E, he's got a backup plan and he'll use it to protect his daughter. It's his trump card, Sir, and he'll play it when he needs to."

"If that's true there's no guarantee the Agency will be the one he plays it with."

"No, Sir, no guarantee."

"Then you better get to them first, Brach. The Agency will give you whatever resources you need and fully expect that will you do whatever it takes to keep Gen-E out of the hands of the Russians. You close this, Brach, find them and bring them back."

"Yes, Sir." Agent Brach tossed the phone on the seat and took a deep breath.

Knowing what Jack is capable of, Agent Brach was keenly aware what the future held. It would be a long and painful cat and mouse game, with Jack one step ahead of the Agency. He only hoped Jack would be able to do the same with the Russians. Nilov would show no mercy if he got to Jack and Becca first; the Russians wanted Gen-E and anyone that stood in their way was expendable. What Agent Brach didn't count on was the nine long years before the Agency would get close to Jack.

CHAPTER 10

ONLY THE SOUNDS of the stroller wheels and Becca's footsteps could be heard in the solitude of the evergreen-lined rural country road. Becca loved morning walks and the tranquility of this far removed corner of the country. Pierce, Idaho, was special for Jack and Becca and somewhere they wished they could have stayed to raise their daughter.

As Sharpe had promised, Laura Neumann took good care of Becca during the end of her pregnancy and delivered the baby in complete seclusion. Keeping true to their family heritage, Jack and Becca named their daughter Marie Lyn Donavon, keeping Lyndon hidden in her full name. It was the first of many names she would know throughout her lifetime.

They never called anywhere home for longer than a few months. Moving would ensure their safety and keep the Agency and Nilov at arms-length. Becca came to understand that a visit from Sharpe would lead to another move within a week. It became so obvious that the minute Jack would tell her he was going to meet Sharpe, she would have the house packed by the time Jack came home. It was Sharpe that would be their constant guardian angel, the one who would monitor Nilov and the Agency and alert Jack when either was getting too close.

Jack would leave the day after meeting with Sharpe to scout out their next location. He carefully selected rental houses with at least an acre of land, on dead-end roads, in sparsely populated small towns. He would walk the properties to make sure the surrounding land offered escape routes if the road was not an option.

Within days of moving, Jack would have the house secured, the surveillance cameras in place, and the escape routes carefully planned. They would walk each route until every possible obstacle was identified and overcome, and the paths were committed to memory. Spending hours researching the area, Jack would get to know everyone who lived there so he could easily identify anyone that didn't belong.

Jack was committed to teaching Becca how to protect herself. They worked daily on hand-to-hand combat, evasive maneuvers and weapons training, and the consistent strength building schedule had Becca in the best shape of her life. If she were to ever find herself in a compromising situation, it was important to Jack that Becca be able to react with instinct rather than panic.

Raising Marie with the knowledge that she was in constant danger made it difficult to portray a normal family. Becca and Jack found every way possible to give Marie as normal a life as possible, allowing her to attend school even though it meant she would only be there for a few months at a time.

When she was young, Marie was unaware that other kids didn't live like she did; she had no idea that people kept the same name their whole life, or that they lived in the same place for a long time. Moving and changing their name was normal to Marie, but as she got older she began to ask questions.

Marie wondered why she was always the new kid in school; why she only participated in sports that didn't have teams; why her Mom and Dad allowed her friends to visit, but never allowed her to go to their house; why she had to memorize a new name and the made up stories of where she came from; and why she wore a military dog tag instead of a necklace like other little girls.

Jack and Becca carefully planned for the time Marie would start asking why, and with all the publicity around prepping for disaster, it was the perfect cover. Being preppers allowed them to explain much of their way of life, giving Marie the answers she needed to accept their way of life.

Years of fencing, taekwondo, archery and rock climbing would teach Marie the skills she would need to defend herself. Although Marie looked forward to Saturday mornings with her Dad and driving a yard kart to check the surveillance system around the property, it was truly meant to be training for her.

Jack made sure Marie felt comfortable with their way of life and wanted her to grow up knowing how to protect herself.

Hours of hiking the escape routes with her Mom made Marie feel at home in the woods. Each Sunday morning Becca would pack a bag with snacks and drinks and they would hike the paths, metal detectors in hand, looking for buried treasure along the way. Not even realizing it, Marie was committing the paths to memory, learning from her Mom about nature, wildlife, and how to navigate the unmarked wilderness.

Sunday morning treasure hikes always ended the same, with Marie running in the house to show her Dad what they had found that day. It didn't matter if it was a bottle cap or an old coin worth two-hundred dollars, each piece had the same value to Marie. Knowing how hard moving was for Marie,

Becca promised her they would find treasure wherever they go.

Jack and Becca didn't take Marie to public places too often, but when they did, it was an exercise in survival. Although Marie thought it was a game, Jack and Becca were very calculated in how they approached these public outings. They would find a place to sit that would allow them a clear view of the entire crowd, making sure to know more about what was behind them than in front of them. Jack would help Marie identify at least two ways out of the crowd and the best paths to get there without being seen.

Scanning the crowd, they taught Marie how to profile people from all walks of life and how to identify potential threats, and more importantly, how to identify who in the crowd would be most likely to help her if she was in trouble.

As she got older, Marie would pick where they sat, explain the escape routes, identify threats, and point out the most likely person to help her before Jack or Becca had time to ask. Jack was confident that if Marie found herself alone, she would be able to find help. Like everything else in her life, Marie thought it was normal. She was completely unaware of the relevance of these games, but would soon find out what she had been taught was more important than she could ever imagine.

Making a trip to the store to pick up a new tire for the yard kart would be boring for most six year old girls, but Marie loved to run errands with her dad. She would jump in the truck as soon as she heard him say he was going to town. She knew it meant she would be able to pick out a treat, and no matter how many times he said no, her dad would always give in. Marie would make sure to eat the candy bar before they got home so she and her dad wouldn't get in trouble for spoiling her appetite.

Marie barely waited for the truck to be in park before hopping out and running into the store, making a beeline for the candy aisle. Jack paid for the tire and her candy bar and this time, Marie didn't even make it out of the store before taking a bite.

"Hey there, wait till we get in the truck, or at least out of the store."

"But Dad, it's my favorite," Marie said as she tripped and fell on her untied shoelace.

"You okay, sweetie?" he asked, helping Marie up to her feet.

"Yep, and I saved the candy bar, see," Marie proclaimed as she held the candy bar above her head in triumph that she never let it hit the ground.

"You did good, kiddo."

As Jack looked at the candy bar held high above Marie's head, a handmade sign on the wall just behind Marie caught his eye.

Remote Historic Cabin for Rent

Enjoy the best of the Northern Rocky wilderness!

Completely updated remote mining cabin with beautiful views of the surrounding mountains.

Bring your mining gear and explore the tunnels in search of gold! This is one of the BEST locations for hikers and nature enthusiasts.

Nearby climbing peaks for beginner and experts!

Weekly rentals Spring through Fall.

The contact phone number was written on a dozen little pieces of paper at the bottom of the sign. Jack reached up and took the entire sign off the wall and walked out the front door.

CHAPTER 11
Marie's Story

THE DREAM WAS ALWAYS THE SAME ... as if I were nine years old again. I can see myself standing in the cabin staring out the window, frozen in fear and disbelief. I can hear my dad telling me he loves me and I can smell the dirt from the passageway. I remember the sound of the leaves crunching beneath my feet as I ran through the woods and I can see the men that took everything from me. The trip I had waited for was now the nightmare I could not forget.

The late afternoon sun was barely peeking through the thick towering pines as we drove up the mountain. The snow was light that winter leaving the river especially low and barely visible in the ravine that ran along the driveway to the cabin. It was my favorite place to be; I was so excited we were going to stay an entire week this year which meant extra hikes with my mom and finally being able to climb Mander Peak.

I had been climbing since I could remember, one-by-one checking off all the cliffs on my list, except for Mander Peak. We had hiked past it many times these past few years and I would beg my dad to let me give it a try. He'd tell me to be patient, that I had to be ready, and this trip I was ready.

There was a sense of calmness at the cabin. I can't put my finger on it but my parents seemed to be more relaxed in this remote corner of the mountains. We were miles from the nearest big city, with only the small town of Northgate between us and civilization.

Mom and I had planned on driving the few miles into town the next day for groceries and a new pair of sunglasses for dad since he sat on his old pair after getting gas on the way up. Northgate General Store had a little bit of everything, from groceries to hardware and auto parts, and it was the only place to shop within 75 miles.

I set my suitcase on my bed and started unpacking, all the while listening to my dad cursing the water heater. It was his usual ritual and I never understood why he just didn't get a new one. It worked only half the time, which meant we took showers and did dishes whenever it decided to heat the water.

I remember walking out to the kitchen as my dad ran the water in the sink waiting for it to get warm, and then seeing him look down at the floor as his socks soaked up the water running out from under the sink. He was so mad he whipped open the cabinet doors and started banging on the old pipes under the sink. That was my cue to quietly leave the kitchen and finish unpacking.

I finished unpacking, listening to the only radio station that had good reception in the mountains. It was a country station, not my favorite, but it was growing on me. Music has a way of bringing people back to a place in time, to a specific memory, good or bad. To this day, I cannot listen to "I Hope You Dance".

As the song ended, I could hear men's voices and couldn't imagine who my dad was talking to; we didn't know anyone up here in the mountains and the nearest neighbors were pretty far away. I remember putting on my sweatshirt and walking over to turn down the radio when I heard a bunch of loud bangs. Guessing it was from my dad's frustration with the sink and water heater, I walked out to the kitchen to see what all the commotion was, but my dad was by himself with his head under the sink.

"Who were you talking to dad?" I asked as I peeked under the sink to see what he was doing.

"No one, I'm just cursing the sink and water heater. Can you open the sliding door curtains and let some light in here?"

"I heard men's voices and then some loud noises." I said as I opened the curtains to the door leading to the second floor deck.

He quickly stood up and looked out the window above the sink expecting to see my mom on the patio below. She had been setting out the chairs around the fire pit for our first night tradition of roasting marshmallows.

With panic in his voice he asked. "Where's your mom, Marie?"

Before I could answer we heard a loud shatter.

I looked down to see my mom lying on the ground next to the broken glass top patio table. She was struggling to stand up when a very big man walked up and kicked her sending her tumbling back to the ground. I couldn't speak; I turned to my dad with tears filling my eyes and looked back outside. He came running just in time to shield my eyes. I heard the shot and deep down inside I knew my mom was dead.

My dad reached for the curtains and yanked them closed; he knew what was coming next. He grabbed my shoulders and looked me straight in the eyes. "We have practiced for this over and over; no tears, no words, just do exactly what you have learned." He pulled up the rug and opened the hatch. "Go! Now! Don't stop, don't look back! I love you, Marie."

He kissed me on the forehead and closed the hatch. I turned the lock from inside as I was taught, grabbed the flashlight and small bag stashed just inside the passageway and started to run. I did exactly as he said. I never looked back.

The passageway opened up to a rocky slope, one I had climbed many times. I knew the way up was safer than the way down, so I climbed to the top and ran toward town.

My dad always told me to run like someone was following me, and although I could not see or hear him, I ran like he was right behind me. It was getting dark and I remember the smell of distant campfires and hearing only the sound of the leaves beneath my feet as I made my way through the woods, stopping only a few times to catch my breath.

I heard the music as I made my way to the clearing on the edge of Northgate and headed for the first building on Main Street. I was dirty from the passageway, my hands muddy and my face lightly covered in a mix of dirt and sweat. There were leaves stuck in my hair and a hole in the arm of my jacket from running through the woods.

I walked in the first open door I could find, ending up in the middle of a bar full of bikers. I had seen biker gangs before, but these guys looked especially rough. Their black leather skull vests and tattoo covered arms were intimidating. I stayed strong and hoped to find someone like my dad's friend, Mr. Sharpe. Out of pure instinct, I scanned the bar for the one person that could help.

"Hey look at this, a little girl in a bar," one of the bikers said as I walked past the pool table listening to the laughter of the other bikers.

I turned quickly and locked eyes with him, provoking his sarcastic response. "Ohhh tough little girl."

One of the women hit him on the back and said, "Come on, Damon, cut the kid some slack."

I turned and walked toward a group of men sitting at a round table in the front of the bar. It was at that moment I saw him, the man I hoped would help. I slowly approached and quietly asked, "Are you the one?"

He laughed. "Depends, kid, the one for what?"

"Hey, JD, she thinks you're an angel," Damon said and the bar erupted in laughter.

I ignored Damon's comment and kept my eyes glued on JD. "I need your help."

He could see I was scared and although his glare was steely and cold, there was a bit of compassion in his eyes. I reached in my jacket and pulled out my dog tag. He held it in his big, rough hand and read the inscription.

> *"I am a special child who finds safety in the goodness of others. Walk by my side and you will be my savior."*

As he was reading, I reached in the purse sitting on the table next to him and grabbed the cell phone, ignoring the look from the woman whose phone I had just taken. I handed JD the phone and turned over the dog tag in his hand. "Here, please."

He hesitated for a minute, but seeing the desperation in my eyes he dialed the number on the back of my dog tag. I watched the look in his eyes change as he listened to the fifteen second recording.

> *"If you are listening to this, then you have my daughter. You have a choice, you can help her or you can walk away. I mean you no harm, but I cannot protect you from those that do. You owe me nothing, but if you help my daughter, I will owe you everything. Take her to a safe place; I will find you. Her life is in your hands."*

JD's eyes shifted from the phone to me and he could see my bottom lip start to quiver as I stared out the window. He turned to get a better look at the black car pulling in the parking lot. My heart was pounding as I slowly backed away from the window. He knew then that I was in trouble, real trouble.

JD stood up putting his hand on my shoulder and gently pushed me behind the jukebox along the wall. He held up his hand like a stop sign, looked down at me and quietly whispered, "You stay right there, kid."

JD watched intently as a man got out of the car and walked toward the door. Giving a nod, the gang knew what JD meant. Damon and a few others walked toward the door as Binovich walked in.

"You lost, mister?" Damon said leaning up against the bar with his arms crossed and a slight smirk on his face. The bar was quiet now and everyone was watching.

Binovich looked around, he was out of his element and knew had no power there. His time in the States lessened his Russian accent, but it was still evident as he looked at Damon and said, "Just looking for my daughter. She seems to have wondered off and I'm worried about her. She's only nine years old."

Damon laughed at the Russian. "Now what in the hell would make you look in a bar for your nine year-old daughter?"

Binovich walked up to Damon, standing just inches away staring directly in Damon's eyes. He reached in his pocket and pulled out a card. "You see my daughter, you be sure to call me," Binovich said as he slipped the card in Damon's front pocket.

Damon didn't flinch; he just stood there staring back at the Russian. Binovich backed up a few steps and looked around the bar. "Any of you see my little girl, you let me know, and I'll make sure to thank you for your trouble."

No one responded as Binovich walked out of the bar. JD watched as the car drove out of the parking lot and headed east, toward the freeway. He looked down at me and held out his hand to help me up. "Come on, let's get you cleaned up."

The second I knew he was going to help I felt the need for self-preservation diminish, and the emotions of the little girl I was were evident by the tears welling up in my eyes. I wiped the tears and looked up at JD. "We need to go, we need to go now!"

"We're not going anywhere, kid; those men are out there looking for you."

I pulled my hand away from his and grabbed the dog tags from his other hand. "Those men killed my mom, we need to find my dad. He needs my help. I'm going to help him."

I turned and began to walk away when JD grabbed my sweatshirt to stop me. "Hang on a second, kid, where's your dad?"

"At the cabin, up on the mountain," I said tugging on his arm to let go of my sweatshirt.

"Damon, Biggs, you two come with me, the rest of you stay here and let me know if that piece of shit foreigner comes back." JD picked up a jacket and helmet and handed them to me. "Let's go help your dad, kid."

We pulled up to the cabin and JD motioned Damon and Biggs to go around back. It was eerily quiet. "You wait here." JD whispered as he got off his bike and walked toward the house. JD pushed open the front door and walked inside as Damon and Biggs made their way up the deck stairs and in through the back door.

Biggs looked at JD. "The kid's mom is out back, they did a number on her. She didn't have a chance. Those Russians are cruel bastards."

Damon pointed to the feet he could see on the floor, just behind the couch. They walked over to find Jack lying on the floor, a gunshot to the chest and his face badly beaten. "They got him, too. Shit, no kid deserves to see this." JD said as he started to walk away.

Jack grabbed JD's ankle. "Where's my daughter, is she okay?"

"Holy shit, he's alive," JD checked Jack's pulse, "barely, but he's alive."

He leaned down closer to Jack. "She's fine, she's with us. Call the cops, Damon, this guy isn't going to last much longer."

Jack used all his strength to reach up and grab JD's shirt. "Keep her safe, keep her hidden. I will find you." Jack reached in his pocket and handed JD his cell phone. "If I don't make it, speed dial number two, he'll know what to do. Now get out of here, she's not safe here."

CHAPTER 12

I HELD ON TO JD as he drove down the dark mountain road. We were just a few miles away from the cabin when we heard the siren of the oncoming police car.

"Look away," JD said as he pulled over and watched the car go by. He looked at me in the rearview mirror. "They'll help your dad."

I held on just a little tighter as he pulled back on to the road. We wound our way through the tree-lined roads for over an hour, stopping only once at a bridge over a deep gully. JD tossed the phone he had used to call the number on my dog tag and we kept moving. I could feel the bike slow down and watched as we turned on a long gravel road that led to a little white house sitting on the river. There was one car parked near the back porch, and a small fishing boat docked along the shore. Big trees towered over the little house making it seem all that much smaller.

"You live here?" I asked.

JD helped me off the bike. "No, but you'll be safe here until your dad gets better."

An older woman walked out the back door wiping her hands on a kitchen towel. "Well look here, aren't you just adorable."

"I'm Marie," I said as JD and I walked up the steps to the back porch.

"Nice to meet you, Marie, I'm Ms. Joyce. Now how did you find your way here with JD?"

JD quickly stepped in. "No questions, Joyce, it's better if you don't ask any questions."

Ms. Joyce looked down at me then back at JD. The look on JD's face was enough to let her know not to prod any further. "Well come on now, let's get you cleaned up. You like cookies?"

"Yes, I do," I answered as we made our way to the kitchen.

"Well then you came at the perfect time. I just took chocolate chip cookies out of the oven."

Ms. Joyce and I walked back outside with a plate of cookies, I handed JD a cookie and sat down on the bench next to him.

"Who were those men, Marie? Why were they looking for you?" JD asked.

"I don't know who they are. Is my dad going to be okay?"

"He's in good hands now; those doctors will fix him up. We'll stay here for a couple days if that's okay with Ms. Joyce, then we'll go check on your dad." JD looked at Joyce who nodded her head in agreement.

"I'll need some help with that boat house while you boys are here. Oh, and that darn car of mine won't start sometimes, see what you can do with that, too," she said as she looked at me and winked.

Ms. Joyce took good care of me, making sure I ate three meals a day and didn't watch too much TV. The guys fixed her car while Ms. Joyce and I drank lemonade and watched them work. She had to scold Biggs and Damon a few times for using foul language, reminding them I was only nine and shouldn't be listening to that kind of talk.

Ms. Joyce taught me how to make corn bread and one night I helped her with dinner. The guys were gushing with compliments, but I knew the lumps in my mashed potatoes were a surprise especially since there would never be a lump in Ms. Joyce's potatoes. Even so, the guys made me think it was the best dinner they had ever had.

I cleared the dishes and brought out the chocolate cake Ms. Joyce and I had made for dessert. It was unusually quiet in the dining room and all the guys were smiling. I looked around wondering why it had suddenly gotten so quiet and then I saw the bag sitting on my chair.

"Go ahead, kid, open it," JD said taking the chocolate cake and setting it on the table.

I opened the bag to find new pants, shorts, a few shirts and a bright orange sweatshirt with a smiling sun on the back. At the bottom of the bag was a new pair of tennis shoes, perfectly white with pink shoe laces.

"We thought you could use those and Ms. Joyce gave us a list," Biggs said.

JD pulled out a bag from under the table and handed it to me. I could see an ear poking out of the top and quickly pulled out the softest stuffed dog I had ever seen.

"Thank you, I love him," I said hugging the stuffed animal.

"That wasn't on the list," Ms. Joyce said smiling at JD.

"Nope, but I saw it and knew it needed a friend." JD leaned over and patted the stuffed dog on the head.

"Thank you JD, thank you Biggs, thank you Damon." I went around the table hugging each one of them.

"What are you going to name him?" Ms. Joyce asked.

I held the stuffed dog close and softly responded, "DJ, that's what his name is, DJ."

Ms. Joyce looked at JD, seeing a sparkle in his eyes she hadn't seen in a long time, "That's a perfect name, Marie, just perfect."

DJ was my constant companion, I slept with him, I ate with him and I took him everywhere. We spent a lot of time on the porch watching the guys work around the yard and tend to the boathouse.

I was sitting on the swing with DJ next to me watching the guys finish up the paint on the boathouse when Ms. Joyce hollered from the back door.

"JD, you all better come have a listen."

Ms. Joyce had the news on the TV. "Is that your cabin?" she asked.

I couldn't say a word. It was our cabin; I listened as the lady on the news reported a woman had accidentally shot her husband in an attempt to kill a bear and that the bear killed the woman. Everyone was silent, staring at the TV in disbelief.

"JD, is my dad dead too?"

"You know what they are doing, don't you?" JD asked. "They are trying to cover this up."

Ms. Joyce looked at JD, "There isn't anyone with that kind of power, except the government."

"Yeah," Biggs said. "But that makes no sense; the guy looking for Marie wasn't American."

"Ms. Joyce, we're going to take a little ride, watch the kid for us."

JD knelt down and wiped my tears, "Hey, kid, we're going to check on your dad, you hang out here with Ms. Joyce and we'll be back soon." JD, Biggs and Damon climbed on their bikes and were gone.

Ms. Joyce turned off the TV and suggested we get some fresh air. Sitting on the swing she held me close, telling me it would be okay and that JD and the guys would find my dad. We quietly watched the sunset listening to the frogs and crickets get louder as the sky grew darker.

Ms. Joyce was so kind, always smiling and trying her hardest to make everyone feel better. The years showed heavily in the wrinkles on her face and hands, but her kindness made her as beautiful today as she was when she was young.

The photos lining both sides of the hallway told the story of her life. She was married young; her husband was a big man with the same tough look as JD. They traveled a lot on the motorcycles that now sit in the shed, covered in a thick layer of dust. A small rose was barely visible on the gas tank of the smaller bike that must have belonged to Ms. Joyce.

"You know, Marie, JD had a little girl about your age," Ms. Joyce said with a warm kindness in her voice.

"I didn't know that. Where is she?" I asked.

"Well honey, God works in mysterious ways; she and her mama were killed in a bike accident a few years back. She was a lot like you, a tough little girl with a heart of gold."

I looked up at Ms. Joyce to see a tear in her eye, "Is that why he's so nice to me?"

"Oh honey that could be part of the reason, but despite his tough appearance JD has a big old soft spot for kids, always has. He is very protective, too, won't let nothing happen to you if he can help it. Come on, Marie, it's getting dark and a bit chilly out here. Let's go back inside and I'll make you a nice cup of hot chocolate."

It was then that I knew JD was her son and the one photo of her with a small boy must have been taken when JD was young.

"Why don't you have more pictures of JD in the hallway?" I asked squeezing her hand a little bit.

"You sure are a smart little girl," Ms. Joyce responded as she looked down at me and smiled. "He is very cautious about associating himself with me. He thinks that I am safer if there aren't any obvious connections between us."

Ms. Joyce sprinkled marshmallows on top of my hot chocolate and sat next to me as we waited for JD.

CHAPTER 13

AGENT BRACH WAS STANDING at the grill on his patio seasoning the steaks his wife had brought home from the butcher that afternoon. It was a Sunday ritual for the agent, grilling steak, watching the game, and drinking a few beers. He avoided work at all costs on Sundays; it was the one day of the week he disconnected from the Agency. This Sunday would not be the same; he closed the grill lid to see the sergeant standing there, a bit nervous knowing it was taboo to show up at Agent Brach's house on a Sunday.

"Sorry for the interruption on a Sunday evening, Sir, but you need to take a look at this."

Agent Brach paused for a moment, finally taking the file from the sergeant and sat down at the table. The first page displayed a photo of Becca; his heart started to race and the shock was clearly evident on his face as he read DECEASED stamped next to her name. He put his hand to his forehead staring at the picture of Becca. "They got to her first," he said, "my God, why weren't we able to find them first?" He quickly flipped the pages to see a photo of Jack with MISSING stamped next to his name. "And the girl?"

"No sign of her, Sir, no sign at all," the Sergeant replied. "There was a lot of blood inside the house; it came back as Agent Lyndon's. We checked the hospitals in the area and there was a Jim Donavon admitted five days ago with a gunshot to the chest. We're pretty sure it's him. Your plane is waiting, Sir. We'll be in Northgate first thing in the morning."

"This happened five days ago and we are just finding out about it now?" Agent Brach asked with obvious irritation in his tone.

"Yes, Sir, the area is fairly remote and local law enforcement is spread pretty thin. They are working on older systems; it takes a few days for the info to show up on the radar."

"That's unacceptable, Sergeant, completely unacceptable. If the Russians got to them then it's a tragedy we can't do the same in our own country."

Agent Brach was angry. He had spent the last nine years looking for Jack and Becca. He knew it would be difficult and always had the Russians in the back of his mind, but never imagined they would get to Jack and Becca first and certainly never expected them to kill Becca. His friendship with

Becca's father fueled his determination to find them, but the Agency steadily cut back his resources as the years went by.

Agent Brach closed the file and glared at the sergeant, "This is what happens when the Agency finds other priorities, other places to spend the money. This is what happens when you try to find a rogue agent as good as Jack with your hands tied behind your back. I'll be damned if I let the Agency stand in my way now." Agent Brach stormed in the house, packed his suitcase and handed it to the sergeant. He waited for the sergeant to walk outside before opening the locked silver case from under his bed. The last time Agent Brach used this gun was the day Becca's father died.

His memory was so vivid that Agent Brach could recall every last detail as if it happened yesterday. The Agency stood in his way then, as they had for the last nine years, and the result was the same. First it was Becca's father, and now Becca that paid the ultimate price for the Agency's lack of resources.

She would never know what really happened to her father, but Agent Brach knew the truth, he knew exactly what happened; he was the only agent with her father that day. Jack was out of commission in the base hospital and the Agency refused to assign another agent, dismissing the fact Nilov was a threat to the Gen-E Project.

Binovich had traced Becca and her father to New York, following their every move until the Agency realized they were being targeted and ended their trip early. Tracing Binovich back to Russia, the Agency believed the threat level was low and sent Becca's father to Italy with Agent Brach as his only protection.

It was there, on the way to the Italian Genetic Research Lab that Nilov's men set up the intercept. Surrounding the car, Binovich demanded they turn over Gen-E, but the doctor had nothing to give them, he couldn't hand over Gen-E. Binovich and his men searched the vehicle, Agent Brach, and Becca's father, but found nothing. There was no laptop, no microchip, no briefcase, no files and no sign of Gen-E. Binovich grew irritated, pointing the gun at Agent Brach; he looked at Becca's father demanding he turn over Gen-E.

As Becca's father slowly lifted his hand, Agent Brach yelled for him to stop, but Becca's father was a good man and he would rather sacrifice himself than allow his research to take Agent Brach's life. Pointing at his head he told Binovich Gen-E was there, in his head. Binovich moved his aim from Agent Brach to Becca's father and told him to get in the front seat of the car.

Agent Brach heard the sniper rifle and watched as the Russian standing at the back of car grabbed his chest and looked down to see the blood soak through his shirt. The Russian fell to the ground, his gun discharging as it hit the gravel road. Two more shots rang out and the two other Russians were down. Binovich, now left alone and unsure where the shots came from, jumped in the driver's seat and sped away.

Lying on the ground was Becca's father. The shot from the Russian's gun had hit him square in the chest and he was moments away from taking his last breath. Looking at Agent Brach he spoke his final words asking the Agent to watch over Becca. As Becca's father took his last breath, Agent Brach looked up to see Sharpe standing there with his sniper rifle. The Agency had sent Sharpe after hearing increased chatter about a possible threat to Becca's father, but it was too late.

It was the Agency's decision to tell Becca her father died of heart failure. Agent Brach wanted to tell Becca the truth, but knew that no good would come of it.

The sergeant knocked on the open door startling Agent Brach back to the present, "Coming, Sir? The plane is waiting."

"Yeah, I'll be out in a minute. Put this case in the trunk."

Agent Brach handed the sergeant his gun case and stood there while the sergeant walked out the front door.

Talking to Becca's father as if he were standing in the room, Agent Brach made a promise, and unlike the promise he made to watch over Becca, this one he intended to keep. "I failed you and I failed your daughter, but I swear on my life that I will stop at nothing to make sure your granddaughter is safe." Agent Brach loaded the magazine in his gun and walked out the front door.

On the way to the airstrip the sergeant explained how the scene at the cabin had been neutralized, which was easy enough to do in such a remote location. The Agency had met with the sheriff and given the directive on releasing the story to the nearest news affiliate, about 75 miles away. It was a very different story than what actually happened, but the Agency could take no chances on exposing the truth.

"What condition is this Donavon guy in, and how sure are we it's Jack?" Agent Brach asked.

"He is expected to pull through and from what our sources tell us, he shouldn't be released for at least another week. We're confident it's Jack, Sir," the sergeant responded.

"Get the doctor at that hospital on the phone now, Sergeant," Agent Brach ordered.

CHAPTER 14

JACK WAS GETTING BETTER and gaining strength, but kept how good he was feeling hidden from the hospital staff. He would act completely incoherent when the doctor or a nurse was in the room to avoid questions about the gun shot, about the death of his wife, and especially about his daughter.

Jack would wait until late at night when the nurse was tending to other patients to walk the hallways of the small hospital. He was trying to gain strength, knowing it was just a matter of time before he would be strong enough to leave. Jack was passing the doctor's office when he overheard him talking on the phone.

"Mr. Donovan is doing better, Agent Brach, he took a shot gun round to the chest and a bullet grazed the left side of his head. He is sedated and resting comfortably. I don't expect he will be going anywhere anytime soon."

The doctor paused for a moment listening to Agent Brach, then responded with a bit of frustration is his voice, "Agent Brach, this isn't the big city, we only have one sheriff and he's managed to get up here once since this happened, and no, we don't have any deputies to post outside Mr. Donovan's room. I assure you he isn't going anywhere, but just so you feel better, I'll give him something to make sure he'll be laying in that bed when you get here in the morning."

Jack made it back to his hospital bed just as the doctor walked in and could see the syringe in the doctor's hand. Jack tucked the IV line under the blanket and crimped it after the doctor added the sedation medication to his IV. As soon as the doctor left the room, Jack ripped the IV out of his arm.

He waited for the doctor to make his final rounds and leave for the evening. Jack knew he only had a small window of opportunity to get out of the hospital unnoticed. The nurse on duty would be checking patients every hour, and if he timed it just right, he would be able to get out of his room, get her keys and be gone before she ever noticed.

Jack was listening while the nurse checked on the patient in the next room when he heard a commotion down the hall and saw the nurse run past his room toward the front doors. Jack got up and looked down the hall to see two men holding up a third man with blood dripping down his face. The nurse took them into the exam room and closed the door.

Jack quickly got dressed but was seeing double as he bent down to tie his shoe. The small amount of sedative that made it through the IV line was making him light-headed. Jack knew he had to focus or he would miss his opportunity to get out of the hospital. He managed to tie one shoe and was working on the second when he heard the footsteps approaching his room. He stood up and staggered toward the door.

"Jim, Jim Donovan," JD called out in a loud whisper.

"I don't know if he's still here," Damon said as they got a few steps closer to Jack's room.

"We got to find him before anyone else does," JD whispered.

Jack recognized the voice; it was the man from the cabin, the one who had Marie. Jack staggered out into the hallway, but before he could say anything, he started to sway, leaning up against the wall to catch his balance. JD and Damon could see Jack wasn't going to make it out of the hospital on his own; they grabbed him and helped him out the side door.

JD helped Jack on the bike and propped him up against the back rest, riding carefully on the country roads back to Ms. Joyce's house while Damon stayed back and waited for Biggs to come out of the exam room.

"That was some good acting in there, Biggs," Damon said as he pointed to the two stiches on Biggs forehead. "Does it hurt, big guy?"

"No, and you're an ass, you didn't have to hit me that hard. Did you at least get the kid's dad?" Biggs asked.

"Sure did, they left about a half hour ago," Damon said as they got on their bikes and headed back to Ms. Joyce's.

I could hear the unique sound of JD's bike turn down the gravel road. As they got closer I could see someone was riding with him, but I couldn't tell if it was Biggs or Damon.

"It's my dad, Ms. Joyce!"

I ran out of the house so excited to see my dad. He was alive and he was here. JD got off the bike and caught my dad from falling on the ground. "What's wrong? What happened to my dad?"

"He's still in pretty bad shape, kid. We need to get him inside," JD said as he and Ms. Joyce helped my dad into the house.

I sat by my dad's side for the next three days, patting his forehead with a wet washcloth and giving him sips of water. He didn't know where he was and I'm pretty sure he didn't know I was there. I was sitting in a chair next to my dad with my head on the side of his bed when I felt him grab my hand.

"Dad!" I said it so loud that JD came running in the room.

"Hi, honey. Have you been taking care of me this whole time?" he asked.

"Yes, I have. Do you feel better?"

"I do, only because you took such good care of me. Come here, give me a hug. I'm sorry, sweetheart, I'm sorry you had to go through this," he said holding me tight.

"I know Dad," I said as I pulled away to look at him, "I know Mom died." The tears welled up in my eyes, and for the first time I was able to cry, really cry. He held me for a long time, letting me cry and telling me we were going to be okay.

Ms. Joyce walked in with a bowl of soup and a glass of water, "Hello, I'm Joyce. You have a real nice daughter; you've done good by her. Come on, Marie, let's let your dad eat something, and give JD and your dad a few minutes to talk."

Jack listened as JD explained the bogus news story and why they had come to get him out of the hospital. Jack knew if it had not been for JD, Agent Brach would have taken him into custody and things would have turned out much differently.

"JD, you saved her life, and mine, and for that I am forever in your debt. You ever need anything, I mean anything ..."

"Appreciate that, man, but taking care of Marie has been a blessing, she's a good kid. We're not known for charity work, but if you ever need help, you come find me," JD said making sure Jack understood the sincerity of his offer.

"I'll do that, JD, thanks for taking care of Marie; she's all I have left."

JD could see the strain on Jack's face. "Sorry about your wife. Why did they target your family and why are they looking for Marie?"

"The less you know the better, and it's not your fight to fight, you've done enough."

"It may not be my fight, but I'll step in anytime, just say the word," JD quickly responded.

"Can you help get Marie and I out of here, we need to get as far away as possible. The Agency is going to start at a five mile radius and within a few days, they will be knocking on Joyce's door. It's not safe for anyone if we stay."

"The Agency?" JD questioned.

"One of those government organizations the general public knows nothing about. They are relentless. I know, because I was one of them."

"It must have been them looking for Marie, some guy was asking questions the day she came in the bar, the day this all happened."

"Did he have a Russian accent?" Jack asked.

"Yeah, he did, and he was a mean looking bastard."

"He's not from the Agency. That's one of the Russians that killed my wife."

"You are in some serious shit. Come on; let's get you out of here. I don't want Ms. Joyce in any more danger," JD said as he stood up and walked toward the door.

"Wait a second," Jack said, "What was Marie doing in a bar?"

JD smiled. "You raised a smart kid; she knew where to find help."

Leaving JD and Ms. Joyce was hard for me; they were my saviors, my guardian angels. Over the years my dad and JD would keep in touch and every so often they would surprise me.

One summer my dad took me to a carnival in a small town just outside Salt Lake City. It wasn't until we got there and I saw JD that I understood why my dad would drive two hours for a carnival. We spent the day playing games and riding every midway ride at least three times. I slept all the way home surrounded by the fifteen stuffed animals JD had won for me.

I always wished we could have spent more time with JD, but having JD know where I was meant that Damon could find out. JD was careful not to share information with anyone and knew spending time together put all of us in danger.

JD trusted Biggs, but Damon was a wild card. He asked JD enough questions over the years to raise JD's suspicion. JD never let Damon get too close to the truth about us and never shared why he would leave for a few days at a time or where he was going. He knew Damon was capable of using us as his bargaining chip if he ever needed one.

Damon was in some big trouble when he was younger and his older brother, Max, begged JD to let Damon ride them. JD reluctantly agreed, and when Max died of cancer, JD felt responsible for Damon. JD knew Damon couldn't be trusted, but JD's allegiance to Max was the only reason Damon was still around.

Jack was right; the Agency was knocking on Joyce's door two days after we left. Ms. Joyce fed the agents cookies and sent them on their way, giving them no reason to think she knew anything at all.

After weeks of intense searching, the Agency left the small town of Northgate no closer to finding Jack and Marie. Agent Brach took Becca back to Richmond and laid her to rest next to her father.

Finding Jack was now more than a mission, it became Agent Brach's obsession. He followed every dead-end lead, monitored every move Nilov and Binovich made, and kept a watchful eye on anyone Jack was connected to; but it would be another eight years before Agent Brach and Jack would finally come face to face.

CHAPTER 15

LEANING MY HEAD AGAINST the passenger window, I watched as the kids played in the perfectly landscaped front yards of the big old houses as we passed through another small town, and hoped someday I would be able to sit on the front porch of a house just like those.

Each time we packed the car, my dad would patiently listen to me complain about moving again, starting another school, and leaving my friends behind. He would wait for me to finish my protest and remind me that we need to take time to find the treasure wherever we go.

I knew he meant those words and that be believed in them with his whole heart. It was what my mom would always say when we moved. I loved to hear him say it, but it didn't stop the dream of a place to truly call home, a place where we stayed long enough for me to paint my room the color I wanted, put dishes in the cupboards, or hang a picture on the wall.

Every move would start the same; it would take hours to decide exactly who we would be, spending most of the first day going over the details of our make-believe lives. Sometimes it was so real that I would forget who I was leaving behind. My dad was incredibly careful about making sure our stories matched and taught me every trick he knew to glaze over questions that would give anyone more information than they needed to know. When mom was alive, she made it fun; she would make it into a game, but now that it's just the two of us, it just isn't the same.

My dad did his best to make me believe that life was good, and that we had the freedom to be who we wanted to be, where we wanted to be, when we want to be there. I may have been born Marie Lyn Donavon, but my life would change so many times, I was running out of names.

"What was mom's last name before you got married?" I asked.

Dad stared out the front window at the road ahead, waiting a moment before he answered. "Samone, it was Samone."

I looked at him and leaned my head back on the window. "This time, I am Sam."

Another first day, another name, and one more time learning to navigate the chaotic, poorly lit halls of another school. I think this was school number twenty, or maybe it was twenty-one. Didn't really matter, it was my senior year and the last time I had to be the new kid.

It always started the same, the teacher would ask the class to welcome their new student and then introduce me, each time as someone different.

Out of habit, or instinct, I profiled each kid within the first five minutes. The dorky kid, wondering if I am the one new kid that will be just as smart as she is so she has someone to hang out with; the rebel who is hoping I will skip school so he can say it was my idea; the quiet kid who no matter how hard you tried, would never come out of his shell; and then there was the cheerleader who truly believes she deserves all the attention she gets, and her quarterback boyfriend who is going out with her because that's what quarterbacks do.

I felt no need to impress the clueless, sheltered, self-centered students of yet another small town school in the middle of nowhere. I stopped trying to fit in a long time ago when I realized normal kids just aren't normal at all. They are closed-minded frantic young kids just moving along a predetermined path.

The smart kid, Mindy, whose parents labeled her as the perfect child, putting so much pressure on her to do great things, her fingernails are all but gone. The quiet quirky girl, Ginger, whose mismatched outfit was on purpose and her funky multicolored patchwork backpack leads me to believe her parents own the hippie candle shop downtown and fully expect her to run it someday. The cheerleader, Krista, clueless and trying so hard to look the part, who will end up married and pregnant before she hits twenty. Her strong, outwardly over confident, yet so insecure quarterback, Nick, is the end result of the father who pushes his kid to be everything he himself was not. I can see his father now, talking football at the local diner to anyone who will listen to him rave about how great a football player his son is. Then there is the rebel, just another kid trying to find himself and barely making it through high school, but making it none-the-less. Graduating is his ticket out of this small town and into the big city where he can play his guitar in a band in some crappy old corner bar, hoping to be discovered.

"Sam... Sam." Mr. Thompson had to say it twice to snap me out of the self-righteous fog I was in.

"You will partner with Chandler for the semester project which includes a hands-on build and a written essay; he'll fill you in on the assignment." Mr. Thompson looked at me waiting for some kind of reaction; after all, he is a teacher that still loves to teach and desperately hopes he is making a positive impact on his students. He stared just long enough to realize he wasn't going to get any type of reaction from me, then turned and added my name next to Chandler on the project board.

"Breaking in the new kid, lucky you, man," Nick said with a blatantly sarcastic tone.

If that sad excuse for a quarterback knew how incredibly ridiculous he looked, he would have crawled in a locker and never come out. Even more pathetic was the steely glare from his cheerleading sidekick.

I locked in on her stare and whispered, "No worries cheer-girl, he's not even close to being my type."

Krista was obviously insulted by my remark and quickly looked away, fumbling with her pencil as if she wanted to say something in response, but couldn't think of a single thing. If I did anything, I made her think twice if he was even good enough for her. High school kids are so easily swayed by simple comments and hyper-focused on the need to be what everyone else thinks they should be.

Sitting there in the middle of the class full of superficial, naive teenagers, I couldn't decide which one would irritate me less. I pretty much figured the guitar-playing rebel would fully rely on me to carry him through this project. I glanced over knowing Chandler expected me to acknowledge we were some sort of partners. He was looking at me alright, staring was more like it. My lack of reaction usually made people uncomfortable, and they would wait, but when they didn't get any reaction at all, they would look away first. It was my power play and it always worked. Except this time. Chandler held his ground, he didn't look away, and he didn't even flinch when Mr. Thompson called on him.

"Chandler, take Sam to the science lab, show her the model and review the project requirements."

"Yes, Sir," Chandler replied, finally breaking his stare as he reached for his backpack and guitar case.

Turning to me, Mr. Thompson continued, "Sam, this is 50% of your semester grade, and since you are starting late, you will want to catch up as soon as you can."

Just my luck to get paired with the last man standing, he probably figures he can get me to do the essay while he gets to have all the fun building. Rebel boy is in for a surprise, I'm building this thing, whatever it is, and he's writing the report.

Chandler held the door. "You coming?" He asked.

We made our way down the hall toward the lab, silent at first, but I knew the questions were coming. Where are you from? What brought you here? Where did you go to school before? As much as he surprised me by holding his stare and the door, I never expected his first question.

"You're not a guy, are you?" Chandler said in a way you would ask someone if they like pizza or not.

My look must have made him realize I didn't find his question funny at all.

"It's just that Sam is a guy's name, isn't it?" he asked.

Ready to set him straight, I snapped my head to look at him when I saw the slight grin.

"I'm only joking, calm down, I know you're not a guy," he laughed and opened the lab door.

"No way, we're building this?" I stood there looking at the model in the front of the lab. My guard was down now; Chandler could hear the excitement in my voice. "If I would have known this is what we were building, I would have given Mr. Thompson a little more of a reaction."

"A sneeze would have been more of a reaction than you gave him."

I stood there staring at what was obviously a home-made contraption on wheels, above it a sign that said 'Self-Propelled Vehicle'.

"Are you sure you're not a guy?" Chandler said as he leaned against the chalk board with his arms confidently crossed and that slight grin on his face again. "It's just that your name is Sam, and I have yet to see a girl excited about building this thing."

I barely heard Chandler as I set my hand on the top of the seat. It was as if I stepped back in time with my dad, wiping the dirt from my eyes laughing so hard I was crying as I drove us though every mud puddle I could find.

"My dad taught me to drive go karts when I was little, he would have to bribe me with ice cream to get me out of the kart. If it would have had lights, I would have driven all night long," I said as I stood there looking down at the steering wheel.

My mind drifted to one of the late afternoons when I was cleaning the yard kart. Since I drove through all the mud puddles on purpose, I was on kart wash duty.

The look on mom's face was priceless when she saw the yellow and blue flowered shirt and pale pink shorts she had just brought home the day before, barely visibly through the layers of mud. She was standing there staring at me, stunned and speechless when I saw my dad out of the corner of my eye. He raised the hose, aimed it directly at my mom and pulled the trigger. It was another all-out water fight, which my dad usually walked away from completely dry, and once again, we were at his mercy.

He hid buckets of water behind bushes and a second hose under a chair next to the porch. He went from bucket to bucket relentlessly dousing us. We finally gave up and just stood there letting him shower us with the hose. He smiled, handed us each a towel and said he was willing to stop winning all the time when we became worthy opponents. My mom and I promised to create with a plan that would certainly send him to the garage for his own towel.

I looked up at my mom, dripping wet with a puddle slowly forming at my feet and told her I could almost see the flowers on my shirt. She laughed and gave me a big hug, wrapping me in the towel as we walked toward the house. My dad just shook his head and mumbled something about flying solo at the kart-wash again. I turned and smiled as mom led me into the house for a warm bath, clean pajamas, and a cup of hot chocolate.

I'm not sure how long I stood there taking my walk down memory lane, when I saw Chandler looking at me as if he were ready to ask me a question.

"So, he taught you how to drive, but did he teach you what makes them work?" he asked.

"I would eat my ice cream as my dad worked on the karts. One day he handed me a wrench instead of an ice cream bar and I have been working on them ever since."

The bell rang ending another first day. Chandler grabbed his backpack and guitar case and headed for the door, "See you tomorrow, Sam."

"Yeah, see ya."

I stayed there for a minute thinking how easy it would be to do it myself, but thinking Chandler wasn't that bad of a partner and definitely better than any of the other kids in that class.

CHAPTER 16

WALKING UP THE DRIVEWAY I was happy this house was in the mountains, the one place I felt at home, if there was such a place. The house was modest, just a small two bedroom ranch with a detached garage. The white cedar siding was in desperate need of new paint and the towering trees in the front yard needed a good trim job.

The furnishings the house came with looked like they had been there for years. The flowered couch and matching gold swivel recliners were straight out of the 1970's, and the silver and white dinette set looked like it was made for an old time ice cream shop.

The house was big enough for the two of us and perfectly situated at the end of a gravel road shared by just two other houses. I knew my dad was committed to preparing for the worst; it was a way of life for as long as I can remember, but ever since my mom died, prepping became his obsession.

Wherever we moved, he would watch the neighbors for weeks memorizing their habits. He knew what cars they drove, where they worked, what time they left for work, what time they got home, the sound their garage door would make when it opened, and what days they did their grocery shopping. He would immediately walk to the window if he heard a car coming up the road and didn't recognize the sound. He'd watch which house the car went to, write down the plate number and then walk to the neighbor's house to borrow sugar or an egg, just to see who was visiting.

Dad selected this house, as he had every one before, with specific criteria in mind. The house had to be isolated, it had to be on a dead-end road, and it had to have a clear path for a quick departure if the road was not an option. This house had it all, and the fact that the small backyard led to a sixty foot cliff was perfect. Most people would have picked this house for the quiet country road or the view, but my dad selected it for one purpose, safety.

It was just the second day and my dad already had the lines anchored at the top of the cliff. We ran through the plan a dozen times before he felt confident that I would be able to get down the cliff without his assistance.

Our late afternoons were taken up by hikes through the forest at the bottom of the cliff to make sure we knew every potential obstacle. Each route had a different rendezvous point in case we were separated, and each plan had a backup plan.

Within a few weeks I knew every square inch of the property, the surrounding forest, and had memorized every plan. It was the only way I knew how to get my dad to relax, the only way to bring him back to being my dad and not my prepping-obsessed drill sergeant.

Out of all the places we had lived, this was my favorite; being surrounded by the forest made me feel closer to my mom. I loved our treasure hikes through the woods and remember how much fun we would have, but could not bring myself to use my metal detector without her.

Unpacking never took a lot of time; there wasn't much my dad would allow me to keep very long. I had just one box that contained everything I owned, and I would go through the memories of each item before finding a place for it. I kept the stuffed dog JD had given me and one of the stuffed bears he had won for me at the carnival; they always sat in the middle of my bed. My metal detector would get propped up in a corner and stay there until it was time to pack for the next move.

Of all the keepsakes I had, the one that meant the most was my treasure box; it held the special memories of my mom. I remember spending an entire morning shopping for the box and the entire afternoon decorating it. We glued gems and jewels all over the outside and framed a picture of the two of us on the top. The picture was taken the day I found an old watch on one of our treasure hikes. Mom was hugging me and smiling as I held up the watch.

"Almost unpacked?"

"Remember when mom and I found this?" I said holding up the pocket watch that once belonged to an early settler.

"I do remember and can still see the look on your face when you brought it home, you were so proud and had a million questions. Whose was it? How old was it? Did it work? Can we get it fixed? How much is it worth?" He paused for a minute, looking at the watch. "Do you remember what your mom said?"

"The treasures we find are priceless because we found them together and the memories are worth more than the watch ever will be."

Dad gave me a big hug, "She truly believed it, Sam."

"I was always so excited to show you what we found on our treasure hikes," I said sifting through the box.

"I remember when mom and I found this coin, it was the same day we spotted that bear and she never hiked again without a gun."

"She was a good shot, too, she worked hard at it."

"She was good at a lot of things dad. She made the best peanut butter cookies ever."

"You finish unpacking and we'll bake some of those cookies together," he set the watch in my hand and walked out of my room.

Looking at all the things my mom and I had found made me miss her even more. It had been eight years, but I could still hear her laugh and see her smile. I laid down holding the watch remembering the fun we used to have and drifted off to sleep.

The smell of freshly baked peanut butter cookies woke me up. I opened my eyes to see my dad standing there with a plate full of cookies.

"They may not be the best, but I gave it a try," he said.

"Before dinner?"

"Why not dessert before dinner?" he said with a smile.

We sat there eating cookies and talking about mom, our treasure hikes, climbing, and the great times we had as a family. His eyes would sparkle when he talked about her, and as I got older, I recognized the intense love my dad had for my mom and hoped someday I would find that same love.

After dinner that night Jack grabbed a beer and walked out to the garage. He had picked up a new headlight earlier that day and planned on replacing the one that had broken. He knew that getting pulled over for something as simple as a broken headlight could put them in danger.

He had glanced at the box perched on the top shelf above the workbench many times before, but could never bring himself to go through it. The tape had dried out from the years of being stored in garage after garage, and on this particular night, the tape finally gave way allowing the lid to pop open. Jack put his beer down and grabbed the ladder. He took the box off the shelf and set it on the work bench, staring at it for a few minutes before lifting off the rest of the tape exposing the contents inside.

It had been years since Sharpe had delivered the box. Jack asked him to retrieve just the most important things from the house they lived in when Becca died. Sharpe brought Sam's treasure box, metal detector, and just a few of Becca's things which sat neatly packed in the box.

Jack took his time carefully unpacking each item, finally allowing his mind to drift back to his memories of Becca. Stepping back from the work bench, Jack looked at all the things that had meant so much to Becca: a picture of her and her father; a shell she had found on one of their dives; a cork from a bottle of champagne they had shared; the key chain her father had bought for her in New York just a few days before he died; an envelope of family photos; and, the treasure box she had made that held the things she and Jack had found on their treasure hikes. Jack looked through the box remembering where they had found each of the treasures inside, but there was one thing that he did not recognize; a small black square with a rubber band around it holding a note. He took it over to the light on the bench and gently removed the rubber band. The note had faded a bit, but he could tell it was Becca's handwriting.

> *"Dear Jack, If you are reading this, then I'm with my father. Please give my love to Marie, make sure she knows she was everything to me and that I am so proud of her. Be strong for her, she is special in so many ways and I want her to know how much I loved her.*

> *Everything you need is on this chip; it's the REAL Gen-E. I didn't want to put anyone else in danger and I wanted our lives to be normal so I hid this after finding out about Marie. I figured if Gen-E was gone, we could move on. I hope you can forgive me for never telling you, Jack, but in the lab that night in Russia, I synced my phone with my laptop and saved the final formula. It's on this chip use it for good, Jack. Be strong for our daughter, be*

strong for me. And remember: take time to find the treasure wherever you go.

All my love, Becca."

The tears were running down Jack's face as he held the letter. He could hear her voice, he could see her face, and wanted more than anything to hold her in his arms.

CHAPTER 17

As much as I wasn't looking forward to working with Chandler on the science project, he was turning out to be the most normal kid in the class. He had started the project before Mr. Thompson assigned me as his partner and invited me over to see what he had done so far. Of course my dad had a million questions about Chandler, and I am sure did some digging on his own to make sure I wasn't going to some crazy kid's house. Dad would have preferred we build the project at our house, but I assured him Chandler was as normal as they come and he finally agreed to let me go to Chandler's house a few days a week.

Working on the written part of the project was painful for me; I hated sitting in one place for too long and would rather be turning wrenches than writing a paper. It was fortunate for both of us that he preferred writing over working in the garage.

We would meet after school, drive to his house and work in the shop for a couple hours. He lived in a nice neighborhood; the houses were newer and bigger than those in town, each sitting on a couple acres of land. I never saw the inside but the outside was perfectly landscaped with trees lining the driveway on either side leading to the attached garage. Stonework around the patio in the back opened up to a pool and gazebo, and second driveway led to the shop where Chandler and I would spend our time. The shop was used mainly for storing his dad's lawn equipment, a four wheeler, an old car his dad had been working to restore for years, and workbench for times when his dad just wanted some peace and quiet.

Working in the shop gave Chandler and I some time away from the rest of the world. He would sit and watch mostly, helping when I needed a tool or something that I couldn't reach.

The project included the written report, building the self-propelled vehicle, and a demo in the parking lot at school. Mr. Thompson also required we name our project and put together a one-page magazine ad to market our creation. The written part of the project had to include a list of all the parts we used and where they came from, the approximate cost if we were to sell the vehicle, the hours we worked to build it, the dimensions, estimated top speed, and a documented step-by-step process of the build.

Our design was more like a go-kart, low to the ground with a seat that tilted back and could be adjusted for the height of the rider. The pedals and chain were from an old bike Chandler had when he was a kid, the steering wheel came from his dad's old riding lawn mower, and the wheels were from an old red wagon we found in the back of his garage.

While I did most of the building, Chandler sat at the workbench with his laptop documenting each step in the report. His writing was colorful and somehow he made the kart-building process actually sound interesting. He was the one who came up with the name for our project; he called it the Sand Kart. I thought it was sweet that he mixed our names together, taking the 'Sa' from my name and the 'nd' from his name.

When he wasn't writing, Chandler would play his guitar and make me guess which song he was playing. I was amazed at how many songs he could play and how many I actually knew. We both grew up listening to country and a bit of rock, so most of the songs were from artists I had listened to for years.

Chandler was really good with a guitar, and when I first saw him, I guessed he would end up in a cover band at some corner bar in LA, but I was totally wrong. His passion for music was much deeper than playing the guitar; he planned on attending college so he could become a music teacher, and if he had time, write a few songs along the way.

Over the few first weeks our project started to take shape, actually looking like a kart, and our relationship was growing to be more than just friends. I liked Chandler, he was kind, funny and completely accepting of the fact that I didn't talk about my past. He never judged me and I think he liked that I was completely different from the girls at school.

We were off school during one of the teacher in-service days so we decided to work on the project and finish up as much as we could. My dad dropped me off at Chandler's house in the morning on his way into town and made me promise I would stay there until later in the afternoon when he expected to be home.

I was sitting on the floor trying to get the seat to fit the makeshift mounting bracket and was completely focused on finishing assembly so we could paint the kart that weekend. I glanced up at Chandler to catch him looking at me with those incredible blue eyes. He was sitting on the edge of his chair with one leg tucked under and resting his guitar on the other. His stare was a bit intense and I felt the butterflies flutter in my stomach.

"You know, Sam, there isn't another girl in school who would hang out in this garage, much less work on a kart."

My response came out of my mouth before I could even think. "Yeah, I know, but since you're the writer, someone has to build this thing."

He picked up a shop towel and threw it at me and we both started laughing.

"Throwing in the towel?" I asked him, smiling as I tried to hold the seat in place long enough to get the bolt through the mount.

Chandler stood up and walked over to pick up the towel and then gently wiped off the grease I had on my cheek. This time the butterflies were more like jet airplanes flying around my stomach. He was so close to me I could feel his breath on my face and instead of letting him kiss me, I got completely flustered and nervously tried diverting his attention to the kart.

"Here, you try," I handed him the wrench and held the seat as close to the bracket as I could, pushing the bolt through the mount, "just give it a few turns to get it started and I can take it from there." His attention was obviously not on the seat, the bolt or the wrench.

"Ouch!" I yelled as the wrench slipped off the bolt pushing my hand into the edge of the metal frame.

Chandler grabbed the towel and wrapped it around my hand, "I am so sorry, Sam, really I didn't mean it. I wasn't paying attention, I'm sorry."

"It's my fault; I should have had you hold the seat." Looking down I could see the blood soaking through the towel and instantly got light-headed. "Uh, Chandler, I think we need to see if your mom has some stuff to clean this up."

Chandler could tell I was a bit shaky. He put his arm around me and held the towel around my hand as we walked to the house. His mom was very nice, cleaning out the cut and wrapping my hand tight enough to stop the bleeding.

"Sam, you need to have your dad take you to the urgent care. I think you may need a few stitches. Chandler, take her home so her dad can get her hand looked at," she said as she put the final piece of tape on the bandage.

"Thank you Mrs. Banks," I said as Chandler walked me out to the car.

The ride to my house was quiet; I could tell Chandler felt awful and didn't know what to say. He parked the car at the top of our driveway, helped me out of the car and walked me to the door.

"Sam, I am so so sorry."

"Really, Chandler, don't worry about it, I'll be fine and it's just a scratch."

It wasn't just a scratch, but I didn't want Chandler to feel any worse than he already did.

"If you need anything after your dad takes you to the doctor, you let me know and I'll come right over."

I knew he felt awful, but this accident wasn't so bad after all. Watching his reaction and how he took care of me proved just how much he really cared.

CHAPTER 18

I was sitting at the table doing my homework when my dad got home with pizza for dinner.

"Hey Sam, I thought you were going to stay at Chandler's until I got home?"

"Yeah, change of plans Dad. I had a bit of an accident this morning," I said holding up my bandaged hand.

"What happened?" he asked.

"Chandler and tools don't really get along too well. Mrs. Banks thinks I need stitches, she said you should look at it and maybe take me to the urgent care."

I reached for the bandage and started to unwrap it. I only got a few layers off when my dad snapped.

"Wait, Sam!"

He put his hand on top of mine to stop me from taking off any more of the bandage. He took a deep breath looking down at our hands and then up at me, this time with those intense eyes I had only seen a few times in my life.

"What's wrong Dad?"

He just stood there holding my hand with both of his as if he didn't want to let go. He closed his eyes and bowed his head.

"Dad, you're scaring me."

He slowly wrapped my hand back up setting it gently on the table. He turned toward the living room and paced back and forth before sitting in the chair next to mine. He leaned in toward me resting his elbows on his knees with his hands tightly grasped together. I could tell this wasn't going to be a good conversation just by the look on his face.

I listened as he told me everything and I felt as if I was standing outside watching. I felt disconnected from myself, from my world as I knew it, and nothing would ever be the same again.

"Sam, you started walking when you were eleven months old and fell and bumped your head on the corner of the table, your mom said it was bleeding pretty good. When I got home that night she told me what had happened and removed the bandage, but there was nothing there, not even a scratch."

I looked down at my hand, and back at my dad. Without a word, I unwrapped my hand, it was gone. No cut, anywhere. As unbelievable as it was, my dad had to be telling the truth, just that morning I had a cut on my hand bad enough to need stitches, and now it was gone. I couldn't speak, I was confused and scared. The thoughts were racing through my head. How did I never figure this out? How did I go seventeen years without knowing?

"We always knew this day would come and your mom and I always thought we were lucky that nothing major happened that would have raised this question earlier. You remember how your mom and I always covered your cuts and scrapes for a few days because you didn't like the sight of blood? Well, we used that as an excuse for you to always close your eyes while we changed your bandages. In a few days we would take off the bandage and your cut was gone, you just never knew it was gone the same day you hurt yourself."

I sat there wondering if I was dreaming or if what I was hearing was real.

"The look on your mom's face that day you hit your head was complete shock. She looked at me, then you, then me again. Your mom was recreating the scene, walking over to the table and explaining how you fell, where you hit the table, and then pointed at your head and said, 'Really, she was bleeding! There was a goose egg on her forehead.' She must have seen the look of confusion on my face, when she ran over to the garbage and pulled out the paper towels covered in blood. Then she stopped, looked over at me and said 'Oh my God Jack, Gen-E.'"

"Who is Jenny?"

He took a deep breath and held my hand tight. "You're old enough now and need to know, to really understand why we live the way we do."

There were many times I would ask why mom died and his answer was the same every time. He would tell me there are bad people in the world that do bad things and not to worry because he would make sure we were safe. He never allowed the conversation to go any further but I was about to find out that it was me they were after, it was always me.

He spent the next few hours telling me everything he knew about Gen-E and that I was proof that Gen-E existed; the only living connection to the project. He held nothing back.

He walked me through the day at the lab in Russia when Dr. Levin was killed, making sure I understood that mom had no idea she was pregnant when she injected herself. He told me about Nilov and the Russian underground, and how the Agency has been looking for us since before I was born.

It all made sense; I finally understand all the moves, the escape routes, the guns, the secret rooms, the name changes. My parents weren't the eccentric preppers I thought they were. They were protecting me.

"Did they kill mom because of me?"

"No, sweetheart, it's Gen-E they want."

"Am I the only one?"

"Yes, Sam, you are. That's why we never stay in one place too long, that's why we live the way we do."

"Will it ever end Dad? I mean will we ever be able to have the life I see other families have, a real home, somewhere we can be who we are, and not who we want to be?"

"Is that what you want, Sam?"

"Yes, very much."

"I've thought about this day for seventeen years, I've gone over all the possible scenarios, all the options."

"We have options?"

"You are the only living link to Gen-E, but your mom left us an insurance policy. I have the Gen-E formula, and one shot to do this right."

"I thought it was destroyed in the fire, at the lab."

"I thought so, too, Sam, but your mom is watching out for you, even now," he set the small chip and note on the table and watched as I read the words my mom wrote, my eyes filling with tears.

My dad felt an overwhelming sense of responsibility to make it right, to give me the normal life I so desperately wanted.

"Your mom wanted to live a normal life; you want to live a normal life. I am going to do everything I can, Sam," he gave me a hug and promised he would make things right.

CHAPTER 19

After school, Chandler gave me a ride home, stopping on the way to grab ice cream at the Diner. It was Friday and we were both happy the week was over and our project was almost done. We sat in the booth eating our ice cream going over our presentation that was due in a week. There were a few small things we had to finish up and we made plans to meet at Chandler's house on Sunday afternoon.

We had just turned on our street when I saw the bike parked in our driveway. I barely said good-bye to Chandler as I hopped out of the car and ran up the driveway barging through the back door.

"JD!" I gave him a big hug.

"Hey kid, who was that dropping you off?"

"Oh, that's Chandler, and don't you dare start, Dad has already interrogated me enough for the both of you."

We sat in the living room catching up and listening to JD tell his stories. If I didn't know JD, I would have thought he made them all up, but knowing him as well as I did, I knew every word was true.

The road was rough on JD, his hair a little more silver than black, his face showing the signs of a tough life, and his voice sounding a bit more tired than usual. It had been a while since we saw JD and never before had he come to our house.

"Sam, JD and I have been talking, and we think it's best if you go with JD for the next couple weeks while I sort this whole thing out with the Agency. You'll be safe with him, think of it as a mini vacation."

"Dad, as much as I would love to be on the road with JD for a couple weeks, I really would like to stay here. Can't JD stay here with me while you're gone? That way I can stay in school and finish the year without falling behind, plus my science presentation is next Friday and I can't leave Chandler to do it alone."

"She makes a good point, Jack; she can't possibly leave Chandler to do the project alone."

"Very funny, JD, it's more than Chandler, I'm so close to graduation."

I know my dad, and as he sat there running the new plan through his head, I could see it in his eyes.

"JD, are you comfortable staying here?" he asked.

"I don't see a problem with it, might be nice to have a little stability for a few weeks and you know Damon, he's gone and gotten himself in some trouble again. He's got the eyes of the law on us now, so hanging out here for a while isn't such a bad idea."

"Alright, but let's go over a few contingency plans in case this location gets compromised."

I gave my dad a big hug, "Thanks Dad! I know it's hard for you to change plans so last minute, but really, JD and I will be just fine."

During dinner that evening we went over the security system, communications, and locations of all the weapons in the house. JD listened as my dad told him about each neighbor, their cars and schedules, insisting that JD repeat back each detail.

My dad took nothing for granted; he covered every base and left nothing to chance. He had to make sure JD would be able to identify anything that looked out of place, anything that would be a danger to me. JD soaked it all in, offering reassurance that we would be fine for the couple weeks he would be gone.

The next morning, dad and I were standing in the kitchen in full climbing gear when JD walked in.

"Going climbing?" JD asked.

"Yes, we are, and that includes you, JD," dad said.

"Oh yeah, right, very funny, guys."

"Your gear is in the living room, we'll meet you out back," I said with a big smile.

Dad and I walked out the door leaving JD in the kitchen completely stunned and in no way on board with the idea of climbing.

JD eventually wondered to the back yard holding his climbing gear in one hand, a cup of coffee in the other.

"You are the only people I know that need this type of gear for your backyard. So which one of you is going to explain to me how this twisted mess goes on?"

Putting a biker in climbing gear is about as easy as trying to get a tutu on a tiger. But dad and I managed to get JD ready to face one of his biggest fears, heights. After a long morning of teaching him how to repel, he finally made it to the bottom of our backyard cliff. The three of us spent the afternoon walking the paths, going through each wooded route in detail until JD was confident with the different escape plans.

JD and I sat on the porch that evening, watching the sunset and talking about the next few weeks. I was happy he was here; JD was about as tough as they get but deep down inside I know he hurts, he misses his wife and daughter and has felt the pain my father feels. I can only hope I offer him some kind of comfort, and by taking care of me, he is somehow being the father he never got the chance to be.

There was uneasiness that following Friday morning. Dad was leaving and I was afraid for him. I didn't know everything but I knew enough to understand what he was about to do would put both of us at risk.

"I love you Dad," I said and gave him a big hug.

"I love you, too, honey. Good luck today on your presentation with Chandler, you'll be great, I just know it."

He was doing his best to divert my attention to something other than him leaving, but the rock in my stomach was painful enough to make me wonder if he was making the right decision. He was doing this for me; he was doing this so I would have the chance of a normal life. I prayed it worked, for both of us.

CHAPTER 20

The table was set with linen, china, and crystal, the champagne on ice, and the candlelight reflected off the windows of the dimly lit room that would soon be full of friends and family celebrating Agent and Mrs. Brach's 25th anniversary. Guests would be there in a little over thirty minutes to enjoy an evening of great food, friends and a walk or two down memory lane.

Agent Brach was flustered with his inability to tie a tie or get the two ends to be remotely close together, and he couldn't get his mind off the intelligence report he had read that afternoon. Instead of fighting the tie, he opted for a stroll to the garage to grab a beer from the refrigerator and a quick puff or two of a cigarette.

Leaning against the workbench he looked down at his wedding ring and wondered how twenty-five years could have gone by so quickly.

"Hello, Mitch."

Agent Brach, completely startled that someone else was in the garage, dropped his can creating a fountain of beer spray all over his suit.

"Shit, shit, what the hell!" he said grabbing the can off the floor. He stood up to see Jack leaning against the back wall of the garage.

"Getting a little jumpy in your old age?" Jack asked with smile.

"Leave it to you to find me. Hell, Jack, I've only been looking for you for seventeen years."

"You know me, Mitch, once a ghost, always a ghost."

"Yeah, I am painfully aware," Agent Brach paused for a moment to look at Jack, almost in disbelief he was standing there. "I'm so sorry about Becca."

"I know you are, Mitch."

"She is buried here, in Richmond; I made sure she was laid to rest next to her father."

"Thank you for taking care of her, it means a lot."

"I'm guessing you're not here in Richmond to crash my anniversary party."

"I need your help Mitch, I need to end this. Nilov has to be stopped and I want to make a deal with the Agency."

"Oh, hell, Jack, good luck with that. It's different now, the Agency has moved on. In the past eight years I've practically had to sell my soul to get any support from the Agency on the Gen-E Project. I'm pretty much obsolete now, replaced by some pumped up younger version of a special agent. People don't pay much attention to me these days."

Holding up the memory chip Becca had left, Jack confidently said, "Mitch, I'd bet this would change their minds."

"What the hell is that, Jack?"

"Let's just say it's a gift from Becca. It's Gen-E, and it's the final formula."

"Well, well, well... that just might get their attention."

"Here is what I want. I want the Agency to bring down Nilov, and I want them to forget my daughter exists. I want to make sure she will never have to worry about being someone's research project. You help me take down Nilov, you get the Agency to promise to leave my daughter alone and the Agency gets Gen-E."

"Jack, Nilov is barely on their radar, hell I can't even get their attention on the latest chatter."

"What chatter?"

"One of the intelligence agents caught part of a conversation between Nilov and Binovich. The intercept was spotty, they only caught bits and pieces of the conversation, but enough for me to take it up the ladder. But again it fell on deaf ears."

Jack always had a keen instinct for danger, a raw gut feeling that would make the hair on the back of his neck stand on end. That feeling was stronger now than ever before and his tone of voice changed to a low and demanding tone.

"What did they hear, Mitch?"

"Mostly bull-shit, except for a few key words that just didn't fit. Most of the agents wouldn't have picked up on it because in the report it was written like the name Jenny, but I had a feeling they were talking about the project. They said a couple other things, but it was broken sentences and a lot of static; what piqued my interest was the fact they picked up the words, lab and kid. But what threw me off is Cortez, does that name mean anything to you, Jack?"

Jack's heart was pounding out of his chest. "When, Mitch, when did you intercept?"

"Early this morning. Why?"

Jack stepped back, running his hands through his hair and then hitting the refrigerator with his fist. "How could I have left her, how did I let it get this far? Oh my God, Mitch, my daughter is in Cortez, she's in Cortez, Colorado, and Nilov knows where she is!"

"I'll call Phil to get the plane ready; we can be at the airport in twenty minutes."

"You go be with your wife, I'll handle this."

"You are not going alone. If you want me to negotiate a deal with the Agency, you better trust me enough to help, and I need an excuse to get out of this beer-soaked suit."

Jack had to agree; he was very well aware of what Nilov was capable of and knew he couldn't do this alone. Jack waited as Mitch explained to his wife that he had to go.

Jack walked into the house and interrupted Mitch. "We got to go. Now! I just called JD, he's watching Sam. He didn't answer and that means just one thing, he can't answer."

Mitch's wife was in awe that Jack was standing there. "Jack?"

Jack gave Mitch's wife a kiss. "I'm sorry, but I need your husband for a few days."

"I understand, go, go help your daughter." She hugged her husband and told him to be safe. She knew his life had been consumed by finding Jack and there would be nothing that would stand in his way from helping Jack.

CHAPTER 21

AFTER CLASS, MR. THOMPSON pulled Chandler and I aside to compliment us on our presentation, asking if he could use our vehicle as the display in the Science Lab. We were glad it was over and excited to know our kart would be the demo for future classes.

Chandler held my hand as we walked to his car after school, only this time I didn't pull away; instead, I held his hand tight, looking up and smiling at him. I really liked being around Chandler, and working on our project allowed us time to become close without the awkwardness or pressure of dating.

Pulling up to the house, I was happy to see JD's bike in the driveway.

"Want to hang out for a bit?" I asked Chandler.

"Really, you're asking me in?"

"Yeah, come on."

The surprise on JD's face was obvious when we walked in the house. He knew I rarely invited anyone over and that Chandler must be special for me to ask him in.

"Chandler, this is JD, uh, my uncle."

"Nice to meet you Uncle JD," Chandler said, obviously intimidated by JD's size and appearance.

"Now hold on young man. JD is just fine. I can't seem to get used to the uncle part."

JD looked at me and rolled his eyes, bothered that I would introduce him as my uncle and even more bothered that Chandler called him Uncle JD.

"How did your presentation go?" JD asked.

"Thanks to Sam, we got an A+ and the teacher is going to use our kart as the demo for other classes."

"Nice work, sounds like a celebration is in order. How about steaks on the grill for dinner?" JD asked.

"I'm in," Chandler said before I could even say a word.

JD and Chandler talked while I poured a few glasses of lemonade and got the steaks ready for the grill. I was standing at the sink washing the potatoes when I noticed the black car turn onto our road, the windows were darkly tinted and the front license plate was missing. It was a car I had not seen before and knew it didn't belong to any of our neighbors. Reaching up I turned off the water and stared out the window watching the car slowly drive up the road. JD noticed the look of concern on my face and walked to the window. We both stood there, silent, staring at the car getting closer and closer.

"What are you guys looking at?" Chandler asked, but neither of us responded. JD quickly walked toward the back door and grabbed the gun out of the closet "Sam, now, it's time to go now."

I dropped the knife in the sink, and turned to Chandler. "You know how to repel?"

"What?" The look of fear on Chandler's face was evident.

"Do you know how to repel? You know, with a rope, down a cliff?"

"Yeah, why?"

I threw him my dad's gear and ordered him to put it on. "You have less than thirty seconds Chandler, let's go."

Chandler sat there, looking at both of us like we were crazy and completely confused why JD had a gun and I was telling him to put on the climbing gear.

"Chandler, there's no time, either you put on that gear and follow me, or you stay here and die.

You now have twenty seconds," I said as I clipped my harness and headed for my room.

We were down the cliff and dropped the gear at the clearing leading to the northern path. We headed south on the path leading to the highway closest to Chandler's house. I had no idea what would happen to JD, but I knew he wouldn't have come with us even if I begged.

Nilov stayed in the car as Binovich entered the house, walking slowly from room to room. Turning the corner from the kitchen into the living room he saw the tip of the shot gun sticking out from behind the hall door. Binovich slammed all his body weight against the door pinning JD up against the wall. JD pushed back managing to free himself but was no match for the Russian. JD did his best to fight back, knowing Sam's life was on the line. The two struggled with Binovich pounding JD until he could no longer fight back. Propped up against the refrigerator, his face covered in blood, JD looked up at Binovich and spit on the floor at his feet.

"You're a dead man; we don't take kindly to Russians in this neck of the woods."

Binovich stood over JD, mocking him and said, "You should keep your guys on a shorter leash next time. Damon took a measly ten-thousand dollars to tell us where you were, I would have paid him a hundred times that. Doesn't make much sense to me, but it doesn't matter anyway. No fight in that kid, none at all."

With one final blow to the head, JD lay unconscious on the kitchen floor. Binovich searched the house looking for Sam. He slowly entered her room, walking to the open window he scanned the back yard and saw the orange rope tied to a post just above the cliff. He climbed out the window to the edge of the cliff. Looking down he could see the gear that Sam and Chandler had dropped and knew now that Sam was not alone, she had help.

Binovich ran back to the front stopping at Chandler's car to look inside. He pushed the school books to the floor and rifled through the glove box finding Chandlers address on the registration. He walked back to the car to inform Nilov that Sam had made her way down the cliff and into the woods and that she was not alone.

"She is with some kid from school, Chandler, and I know where he lives," Binovich said as he drove away headed for Chandler's house.

Nilov glared at Binovich, "Jack, where is he?"

"Not there, just the biker, and I took care of him."

My emotions shut down, I was in survival mode. It was so automatic that I didn't even realize how focused I was until Chandler yelled for me to stop. I instantly turned around and covered his mouth with my hand, "Shhh, you can't say another word," I whispered in his ear. I couldn't hear anything except the sound of both of us breathing. All the training I went through my entire life was for one reason; it was for this very moment. I was prepared, I was doing everything I had been taught without even thinking, the only difference was, this time our lives depended on it.

"I don't understand," Chandler whispered as I slowly pulled my hand away from his mouth.

"I can't explain now, but I can tell you that this is real, as real as it gets. I'm special, and those men in that car, they are looking for me. I have been trained for this, Chandler, you have to trust me, you have to listen to everything I say and do everything I ask."

I grabbed Chandler's hand and led him along the path, pointing up when we got to the wall. He nodded in agreement and together we scaled the twenty foot outcrop of rock, stopping only briefly at the top to catch our breath. We continued running through the woods when the thick underbrush finally broke, opening to the cut grass along the side of the rural highway that led into town. We crouched in the tall grass waiting for the road to be completely clear of cars before crossing.

"My house is just over that next hill, my parents will help."

"Chandler, we can't go there, if we do, your parents will be in danger. Can you get to your motorcycle without anyone seeing you?"

"Yeah, I think so, but they will hear it as soon as I start it."

"Then you'll have to push it far enough away before you start it."

We watched Chandler's house from the cover of the woods, making sure it was clear. His dad wasn't home from work yet, and we could see his mom in the kitchen.

"I'm going to get the bike and I'll meet you behind the Kemper's house. The old train tracks back there lead into town."

"No, Chandler, we can't go back to town, they will be watching. We need to go to the old mill up on Montrose Road; it's the spot my dad and I picked out. I have supplies there and we will be fine until my dad comes. Make sure your mom doesn't see you, she is alone and we don't want to drag her into this."

Binovich and Nilov watched as Chandler snuck into the shed and walked his bike to the path behind the Kemper's house. They had no way to follow him, but traced the train tracks on the map to see where they led, pinpointing just a few locations Sam and Chandler could possibly find help.

Their first stop was a road-side restaurant; Binovich searched the area but didn't find any motorcycle tracks in the gravel parking lot. Nilov followed Binovich inside to ask if anyone had seen the kids. From inside the bar, Nilov saw the single headlight fly by and continue down the path.

They stopped next at the abandoned quarry, but there was no sign of the bike or the kids. There was just one place left to check, Nilov pointed to map instructing Binovich to drive to the Mill on Montrose Road.

On the plane Jack called JD's phone again; it had been just thirty minutes since he last tried. The ringing phone finally roused JD. He struggled to reach for the phone; he was semi-conscious and his vision was blurred. He tried three times to grab the phone before finally feeling it in his hand.

"JD?" Jack said with panic in his voice.

"Jack, they got away, they got down the cliff."

"What do you mean, they? Who is with Sam?"

"Chandler," was all JD said before he blacked out, dropping the phone on the floor.

Jack looked at Mitch, "She got away, but for how long, I'm not sure. Can you get medics to my house? JD's in bad shape."

Mitch called for the medic while Jack paced back and forth in frustration.

"How long will it take to get a chopper off the ground at Cheyenne?" Jack asked.

"What are you thinking?"

"Sam took one of three routes from the house, each of them having a separate rendezvous point where she knows to wait for me. I need the chopper to do a scan of all three; if they are at any one of them, the infrared will pick them up."

Mitch contacted the base, giving them the coordinates of the three rendezvous points.

"ETA is just under an hour, Jack, when they get there, they'll patch us in."

The minutes ticked by as if time were standing still. Phil was pushing the capabilities of the jet, but they were still over an hour from Cortez. Jack could only hope the chopper would be able to locate the kids, saving time they would have to spend on a ground search.

The call came as the chopper approached the first location. Jack and Mitch were sitting on the edge of their seat watching the screen as the crew scanned the area with no sign of life. Jack studied the map of Cortez, scanning the next two locations. He put his finger on the mill and followed the railroad tracks that led toward town, slowing down as he approached Chandler's house.

"They are at the mill, Mitch. Get the chopper to the mill!"

The mill had been abandoned for decades with most of the buildings in ruins from years of neglect. The main two-story building was constructed to hold the weight of the heavy machines, its large beams and stone exterior offered protection from the elements that devoured the rest of the mill, leaving it the last building intact and the reason my dad selected it as the rendezvous point.

I was holding on tight to Chandler, my arms wrapped around his waist. I would look behind us every few minutes to make sure we weren't being followed. "I see the mill, stop the bike and stash it in the trees."

"Sam, what is going on?"

"Come on, I'll explain when we get inside."

We walked in silence the rest of the way to the mill. I could hear Chandler's breathing, it was heavy and deliberate, he was scared and he had every right to be. He didn't push me, but I knew he wanted to understand why we were running, why those men were chasing us, and why my dad and I needed a rendezvous point at all.

We made our way to the second floor of the mill and Chandler helped move the bookcase exposing a hole my dad had cut in the wall. I reached in and grabbed the backpack.

"Here take this, it will be dark soon, but only turn it on if we absolutely have to," I said handing him the flashlight.

"Sam, I..."

"I know Chandler; you didn't ask for this, you don't deserve to be dragged into this mess. I wish it was different, I wish I hadn't invited you in. If I would have just let you drop me off, you wouldn't be here; you would be home safe."

"Sam, I don't care about being home, or being safe, I care about you."

I looked at Chandler, and for a moment I felt the butterflies in my stomach. It was what I had been hoping to hear from Chandler, but not here, not now. I couldn't let emotion get in the way of what we had to do. Deep down inside I wanted to tell him how I felt, that I cared for him too, but instead I had to focus on what was happening.

We sat in the second floor office of the mill as the light slowly faded into darkness. Chandler listened quietly as I explained who I was, where I came from, and why Nilov was after me.

"I'm not who you think I am," I said.

Chandler reached over, smiled, and held my hand, "You are exactly who I think you are. We'll make it through this Sam, we will."

His smile faded as we heard the footsteps on the stairs. I motioned to him to move to the door on the far end of the office. I grabbed the backpack, pulled out the phone, slid it in my sock and ran for the door.

"Not so fast," Binovich grabbed my shirt and pulled me close, wrapping his forearm around my neck.

"Sam!" Chandler yelled as Nilov stuck a gun in his back.

"No! No! Don't shoot him, I'll go with you, I'll give you whatever you want!" I yelled.

"Of course you will," Nilov said in his thick Russian accent, "What do you suppose I do with him?"

"Let him go, he has nothing to do with this," I pleaded as I struggled to get Binovich to release his grip.

"Now you know it is not possible to let him go," Nilov said with a menacing tone as he walked Chandler out of the office and into the darkness of the main second floor lobby area.

It was dark, but I could see Nilov hit Chandler on the back of the head and kick him. Chandler disappeared into the gaping hole in the floor, and I heard his body hit the ground below.

"Chandler! Noooooo!" I screamed, but there was no response. It was eerily quiet. As strong as I thought I was, I was unable to hold back the tears.

In that moment of silence I could hear the distant sound of a chopper; I struggled hard this time, but couldn't budge the tight hold Binovich had around my neck.

The jet was within thirty minutes of Cortez when the chopper reached the mill. Jack's eyes were locked on the screen as the images came through. It was clear; Jack and Mitch watched helplessly as the two large Russians walked Sam out of the mill and put her in the car. They could see the heat signature of a body lying on the ground and knew it was Chandler.

"We know she's alive, we know where she is and we'll get her back, Jack, I promise," Mitch said.

Jack sat there, feeling hopeless as he watched the car drive away from the mill, "Call off the chopper, Mitch, call them off."

"What? Why?"

"They know the chopper is there, they will do everything they can to run and that puts Sam in too much danger. Call them off now!"

Mitch reluctantly reached for the phone and gave the order for the chopper to stand down, "I hope you know what you're doing, Jack, that chopper was our only sightline."

"I'm banking on all those years of teaching Sam how to take care of herself, and hoping she did exactly what she was taught."

Jack reached for his phone and started the GPS tracker, praying for a signal, but the phone was silent.

Binovich was driving and Nilov watched my every move in the passenger visor mirror. These country roads were familiar to me, and if I was right, we were headed toward the airport. I had to get to my phone, but there was no way to do it without Nilov knowing. These Russians were smart, very smart, and I had just one chance to distract them long enough to get to my phone.

I yelled as loudly as I could, "Look out for the deer!"

Binovich slammed on the brakes and Nilov looked away, bracing himself on the dashboard. I slid my finger inside my sock and hit the power button on my phone, sitting back up before Nilov's stare returned to the mirror.

"I didn't see no deer," Binovich said looking from side to side.

"I did, it ran across the road, just back there," I said, diverting their attention to the oncoming car. "I hope that car doesn't hit the deer."

Binovich turned his attention to the road watching the oncoming car pass and its taillights fade in his rearview mirror.

They were talking in Russian, pointing at the map on the navigation system. I was right; they were headed for the airport. What they didn't know was that the bridge over the river was washed out in the last big storm and the only alternate way to the airport would make them backtrack, adding at least thirty minutes to the drive. I needed all the time I could get for my dad to find me and wasn't about to tell them about the bridge.

As the jet approached Cortez, Jack scanned the blackness that surrounded the small town. His heart pounded as he pictured Sam somewhere in those mountains with Binovich and Nilov. The beep of the GPS locater echoed in the silence of the cabin.

"Mitch, they are just north of Cortez on Railroad Avenue heading west. I bet they don't know that bridge is out and they are going to have to turn around. We can intercept on the detour, we've got them locked in."

"Jack, do you really think a poorly lit road in the middle of nowhere is the best option? I understand you know the area, but that is the last place I would pick to try and get Sam back. You know Nilov isn't going to want to keep Sam on the ground for long, he has to be headed to the airport, and he has to have a plane waiting for him."

Jack thought about it for a minute and knew that Mitch was right. All the different scenarios were running through his head, each of them ending poorly.

"I guess we'll have to make sure his plane is ready to go." Jack grabbed the garment bag out of the luggage compartment and changed into one of Phil's pilot's uniforms. "Find me a picture of Nilov's plane."

Both Mitch and Jack scanned the airport for Nilov's plane as Phil taxied the jet to the hangar.

"There, over there, the jet with the red wing tips, that's Nilov's," Mitch said as he compared the plane to the Agency file photo.

As hard as I tried, I couldn't understand anything they were saying. My dad spoke Russian and tried teaching me, but I never mastered the language. Now I wish I had.

We pulled into the airport hangar; I was terrified and knew that if I got on that plane, my dad may never find me. I grabbed the door handle and the minute the car stopped, I jumped out and started to run for the door. Binovich grabbed my hair and flung me to the ground. With one hand he took my shirt and pulled me to my feet, forcing me to walk toward the plane. I struggled, kicked and pulled, but could not break his hold. He pushed me up the stairs and threw me in the front seat of the plane.

Sitting on the right side, I could see the cockpit and the back of the pilot. He was holding a clip board checking off boxes as he maneuvered the instrument panel preparing for takeoff. I thought if I could get to the instruments I could do enough damage to keep the plane from taking off. I was about to make my move when Nilov sat down in the seat across from me. He was staring shamelessly as if he were proud to have finally gotten his prize. He now had what he wanted, he had me, and he had Gen-E. This was the end of my life as I knew it and I began to cry at the thought of never seeing my dad again and spending the rest of my life with the men who killed my mom.

"You will be well cared for in my country," Nilov said as he removed his jacket.

I glared at him with anger and hate in my eyes, "I'll be a guinea pig, you mean."

"Yes, well, you have your parents to thank for that," he responded coldly.

"My dad will never stop looking, he will find me, and you will wish you left me here," I said matching his steely stare.

"Oh, young girl, that is something I have planned for. Your father is smart and his love for you strong. He will search, but he will never find you."

He changed from speaking English to me, to speaking Russian to the pilot. From his seat, he had to lean forward to see into the cockpit, but could not see the pilot as he gave the order to take off.

"Da," the pilot responded in perfect Russian.

That voice, I know that voice, that's my dad's voice! I turned my head to the cockpit and showing no emotion at all I read the sign he held up on his clipboard 'SEAT BELT SAM!!'.

Without hesitation I reached down and fastened my seatbelt, pulling it as tight as I could. My heart was racing; I was less than six feet from my dad and even less from the man who wanted him dead. I watched as my dad guided the plane to the runway and listened as he revved the engines preparing to takeoff.

The plane began to accelerate, faster and faster. My dad slammed on the brakes skidding off the runway, sending Nilov head on into the wall next to the cockpit door. He lay there at my feet, his head turned in such a way that I knew his neck was broken and he was dead. Binovich flew from the back of the plane to the front, landing on the floor behind my seat. He was standing up, dazed and a bit off balance, when he saw my dad come out of the cockpit.

"You!" Binovich yelled as he reached for his gun, but he never had a chance. My dad didn't hesitate; he shot just once, putting an end to the years of running, the years of being hunted.

"It's over, Sam," he said as he held me close.

CHAPTER 22

EVERY NOW AND THEN, I see the black car with two completely obvious federal agents parked just down the street. They know I see them and have given up trying to hide. It didn't bother me that we were being watched, I knew this time they would keep their distance and it was almost comforting to know that they were there to protect my dad and me.

My attention turned to the kids playing in the perfectly landscaped front yards, but this time it wasn't from a car window; it was from the front porch of the home I always dreamed of.

My dad walked outside, his clothes covered in yellow paint, and his hair speckled in white. I smiled as he sat down beside me on the front porch stairs.

"Thanks for painting my room, Dad."

He gave me a big hug, looking more relaxed than I had ever seen him. He handed me a box with a bow.

"It's not my birthday," I said as I untied the bow. I didn't open the box; I just looked at him waiting for him to tell me why I was getting a gift.

"Go ahead, open it," he said.

I flipped up the lid of the box to reveal the pocket watch my mom and I had found on one of our treasure hikes. It looked new, shining in the sunlight, "You had it restored?"

"Flip it over."

Inscribed on the bottom of the watch was my mom's favorite saying, *Take time to find the treasure wherever you go.*

"You and this house is all the treasure I need Dad."

"So what's our story this time, Sam?"

"Not sure, it's different this time. It's the last time and I want it to be special."

He patted me on the back as he stood up, "I'll grab us some lemonade."

I sat there for a moment remembering my mom. I felt a sense of calm as if she were there, watching over me and telling me it's going to be okay.

A loud bang startled me out of my daydream. Looking down the street, I realized it was just some of the kids with firecrackers. I took a deep breath, unsure if I will ever be able to fully let my guard down, but for now, I'm going to do my best to be a normal small town girl.

Being the 4th of July, it was a perfect weekend to celebrate. We finally have our own sort of independence, and definitely our freedom from Nilov and the Agency.

Sitting on the front porch of our home gave me a feeling of peace until the front gate flew open banging against the fence. Running up the front walk was an adorable little boy in blue shorts, a red shirt and little white baseball cap.

"Hi, I'm Timmy, I am going to find treasure!" he said proudly holding a brand new metal detector.

"Hi Timmy, that's a nice one, you will for sure find treasure with that. Best place to look is in the woods."

His eyes squinted a bit and he looked up at me, puzzled by my comment.

"You know how I know that?"

"How?" he asked.

"I have a metal detector too."

Timmy's big brown eyes lit up and with a gigantic smile he said, "No way!"

"Yes I do."

"Have you found treasure?" he asked.

"Funny you should ask, Timmy, I found this watch a long time ago and my dad made it look brand new for me."

"I hope I find something that awesome."

"You keep working at it and you will, I just know it."

"Hi!" Timmy said as his mom walked through the gate.

She was beautiful and oddly didn't fit in this small town. Her outfit was casual, yet it looked like she just stepped out of a fashion magazine. Her hair was blond and shiny with wisps falling softly in her line of vision. She walked with confidence, yet her smile was soft and welcoming. I wondered what her story was; she certainly was not from around here.

"I'm sorry he just came barging in," she said as she reached out to hand me the basket she was carrying, "These are for you; Timmy and I baked them this morning. Welcome to the neighborhood."

"I'm Jo," she said with a smile, extending her hand.

I shook her hand, "Nice to meet you," and without hesitation said, "I'm Sam."

I couldn't pick any other name. I gained my freedom to be who I wanted to be as Sam, and it was a name that would be mine for a long time, a name that would connect me with my mom forever.

Timmy ran between us with metal detector in hand.

"You'll have to excuse him; he is very excited about his detector," Jo said as she watched him run around the corner of the house. "He has been asking for one for a long time, yesterday was his birthday and it hasn't left his side since he opened it."

"That's okay; I remember how excited I was when I got my first one and I've been treasure hunting ever since."

"Don't go too far Timmy, we need to get you packed," she turned to me and with a bit of frustration in her voice, she added, "He's going to his Dad's in LA for a week after the parade."

Now that makes sense, she is from LA. I should have guessed with the way she was dressed and how perfectly her hair was done for such a warm July day.

"How long have you been here?" I asked.

"Just over a year and we love it, it's perfect for Timmy and since I work from home, I wanted to pick somewhere we could get a fresh start that would give him a real sense of home, and it's safe here."

I smiled and nodded in agreement. She had no idea how much I understood.

Dad walked out the front door with four glasses of lemonade. He must have been watching from inside, and I could tell he had taken a minute to wipe the paint off his face and get as many of the speckles out of his hair as he could.

"Hello, I'm Jack," he shook her hand, holding it just a bit longer than usual, and would have kept holding it had the loud rumble of motorcycles not caught his attention.

We could hear them before we ever saw them, and I knew by the sound, one of them was JD. I looked over at my dad and smiled as I ran toward the road.

Jo yelled for Timmy, but dad put his hand on her shoulder, "Nothing to worry about, Jo, these guys are as good as they come."

I barely gave JD time to get off his bike, giving him a huge hug, "Glad to see you're okay, JD."

"You're not doing too bad yourself kid," JD walked up to my dad and shook his hand, "You're not an easy man to find."

"You know I like it that way, JD."

It was obvious that dad and JD had a strong bond, one that would endure a lifetime. Both would be there for each other, and for me, no matter what.

Jo smiled, tilting her head as if she wasn't exactly sure how these two completely different men would have been friends.

"My, isn't she pretty," JD said as politely stared at Jo.

"This is our neighbor, Jo. Jo, this is JD."

JD shook her hand, and just as dad had done, he held it a bit longer.

"You all staying for the parade?" she politely asked looking at the line of bikes behind JD's.

I'm sure she was a bit intimidated by all the bikes, but by the way she was looking at my dad, I think she was more intrigued by him, and less worried about JD and the guys.

"Unfortunately we'll be on our way soon; we're just passing through, dropping off a little something."

JD didn't say another word. He simply nodded toward the road and right on cue, Biggs drove up the curb and parked on the sidewalk in front of me, tossing me the key as he hopped off the bike.

"Really, JD? Really? This is for me?"

"Sure is, even got your name on it," he said pointing to the gas tank with *id* painted in pink script.

I walked over to the bike and the first thing I noticed was the rose on top of the gas tank. "Is this... did this belong..."

He put his arm around me and quietly answered, "Yes, it did. Ms. Joyce wanted you to have it under one condition. You have to go visit her soon."

"I will, JD, I will!" I hopped on the bike, amazed it was mine. "It's beautiful, JD, thank you, and Ms. Joyce so much."

"There's a helmet hanging on the back, you wear that riding, Kid."

"I will, JD, I promise."

"Well alright then. Jack, it was great to see you, man. Jo, it was a pleasure," JD shook my dad's hand, gave Jo a slight nod, and gave me a big hug. "Kid, you take care now, we'll see you soon."

I watched as they rode down the street lined with all our new neighbors waiting for the parade to start. The daunting sight and roaring sound of the bikes turned every head along the way.

I closed my eyes, gently grasping the handlebars of my new bike and listened as the sound of JD's motorcycle faded into the distance.

Even with my eyes closed, I could tell someone was standing next to me, their shadow blocking the sun. I opened my eyes to see Chandler, propped up on crutches. He looked at me and smiled, putting his hand on top of mine. I slid my hand off the handlebars and held his tight.

This very moment in time was the start of my life as Sam, just a regular girl, living on a small town main street in a house with a big front porch and white picket fence. It was the happiest I had been in a long, long time.